The mate of the Vancouver

Morley Roberts

Originally Published by
STREET & SMITH, PUBLISHERS
1900

Contents

PART I. ON BOARD THE VANCOUVER.

I am going to write, not the history of my life, which, on the whole, has been as quiet as most men's, but simply the story of about a year of it, which, I think, will be almost as interesting to other folks as any yarn spun by a professional novel writer; and if I am wrong, it is because I haven't the knowledge such have of the way to tell a story. As a friend of mine, who is an artist, says, I know I can't put in the foreground properly, but if I tell the simple facts in my own way, it will be true, and anything that is really true always seems to me to have a value of its own, quite independent of what the papers call "style," which a sailor, who has never written much besides a log and a few love-letters, cannot pretend to have. That is what I think.

Our family—for somehow it seems as if I must begin at the beginning—was always given to the sea. There is a story that my great-grandfather was a pirate or buccaneer; my grandfather, I know, was in the Royal Navy, and my father commanded a China clipper when they used to make, for those days, such fast runs home with the new season's tea. Of course, with these examples before us, my brother and I took the same line, and were apprenticed as soon as our mother could make up her mind to part with her sons. Will was six years older than I, and he was second mate in the vessel in which I served my apprenticeship; but, though we were brothers, there wasn't much likeness either of body or mind between us; for Will had a failing that never troubled me, and never will; he was always fond of his glass, a thing I despise in a seaman, and especially in an officer, who has so many lives to answer for.

In 1881, when I had been out of my apprenticeship for rather more than four years, and had got to be mate by a deal of hard work—for, to tell the truth, I liked practical seamanship then much better than navigation and logarithms—I was with my brother in the *Vancouver*, a bark of 1100 tons register. If it hadn't been for my mother, I wouldn't have sailed with Will, but she was always afraid he would get into trouble through drink; for when he was at home and heard he was appointed to the command of this new vessel, he was carried to bed a great deal the worse for liquor. So when he offered me the chief officer's billet, mother persuaded me to take it.

"You must, Tom," she said; "for my sake, do. You can look after him, and perhaps shield him if anything happens, for I am in fear all the time when he is away, but if you were with him I should be more at ease; for you are so steady, Tom."

I wasn't so steady as she thought, I dare say, but still I didn't drink, and that was something. Anyhow, that's the reason why I went with Will, and it was through him and his drinking ways that all the trouble began that made my life a terror to me, and yet brought all the sweetness into it that a man can have, and more than many have a right to look for.

When we left Liverpool we were bound for Melbourne with a mixed cargo and emigrants; and I shouldn't like to say which was the most mixed, what we had in the hold or in the steerage, for I don't like such a human cargo; no sailor does, for they are always in the way. However, that's neither here nor there, for though Will got too much to drink every two days or so on the passage out, nothing happened then that has any concern with the story. It was only when we got to Sandridge that the yarn begins, and it began in a way that rather took me aback; for though I had always thought Will a man who didn't care much for women, or, at any rate, enough to marry one, our anchor hadn't been down an hour before a lady came off in a boat. It was Will's wife, as he explained to me in a rather shamefaced way when he introduced her, and a fine-looking woman she was—of a beautiful complexion with more red in it than most Australians have, two piercing black eyes, and a figure that would have surprised you, it was so straight and full.

She shook hands with me very firmly, and looked at me in such a way that it seemed she saw right through me.

"I am very pleased to see you, Mr. Ticehurst," she said; "I know we shall be friends, you are so like your brother."

Now, somehow, that didn't please me, for I could throw Will over the spanker boom if I wanted to; I was much the bigger man of the two; and as for strength, there was no comparison between us. Besides—however, that doesn't matter; and I answered her heartily enough, for I confess I liked her looks, though I prefer fair women.

"I am sure we shall," said I; "my brother's wife must be, if I can fix it so."

And with that I went off and left them alone, for I thought I might not be wanted there; and I knew very well I was wanted elsewhere, for Tom Mackenzie, the second Officer, was making signs for me to come on deck.

After that I saw her a good deal, for we were often together, especially when she came down once or twice and found Will the worse for liquor. The first time she was in a regular fury about it, and though she didn't say much, she looked like a woman who could do anything desperate, or even worse than that. But the next time she took it more coolly.

"Well, Tom," she said, "he was to take me to the theater, but now he can't go. What am I to do?"

"I don't know," said I, foolishly enough, as it seemed, but then I didn't want to take the hint, which I understood well enough.

"Hum!" she said sharply, looking at me straight. I believe I blushed a little at being bowled out, for I was I knew that. However, when she had made up her mind, she was not a woman to be baulked.

"Then I know, Tom, if you don't," she said; "you must take me yourself. I have the tickets. So get ready."

"But, Helen!" I said, for I really didn't like to go off with her in that way without Will's knowing.

Her eyes sparkled, and she stamped her foot.

"I insist on it! So get ready, or I'll go by myself. And how would Will like that?"

There was no good resisting her, she was too sharp for me, and I went like a lamb, doing just as she ordered me, for she was a masterful woman and accustomed to have her own way. If I did wrong I was punished for it afterward, for this was the beginning of a kind of flirtation which I swear was always innocent enough on my side, and would have been on hers too, if Will had not been a coward with the drink.

In Melbourne we got orders for San Francisco, and it was only a few days before we were ready to sail that I found out Helen was going with us. I was surprised enough any way, for I knew the owners objected to their captains having their wives on board, but I was more surprised that she was ready to come. I hope you will believe that, for it is as true as daylight. I thought at first it was all Will's doing, and he let me think so, for he didn't like me to know how much she ruled him when he was sober. However, she came on board to stay just twenty-four hours before we sailed; the very day Will went up to Melbourne to ship two men in place of two of ours who had run from the vessel.

Next morning, when we were lying in the bay, for we had hauled out from the wharf at Sandridge, a boat ran alongside just at six o'clock, and the two men came on board.

"Who are you, and where are you from?" I asked roughly, for I didn't like the look of one of them.

"These are the two hands that Captain Ticehurst shipped yesterday from a Williamstown boarding house," said the runner who was with them.

I always like to ship men from the Sailor's Home, but I couldn't help myself if Will chose to take what he could get out of a den of thieves such as I knew his place to be.

"Very well!" said I gruffly enough. "Look alive, get your dunnage forward and turn to!"

One of them was a hard-looking little Cockney, who seemed a sailor every inch, though there weren't many of them; but the other was a dark lithe man, with an evil face, who looked like some Oriental half-caste.

"Here," said I to the Cockney, "what's your name?"

"Bill Walker, sir," he answered.

"Who's the man with you? What is he?" I asked.

"Dunno, sir," said Walker, looking forward at the figure of his shipmate, who was just disappearing in the fo'c'sle; "I reckon he's some kind of a Dago, that's what he is, some kind of a Dago."

Now, a Dago in sailor's language means, as a rule, a Frenchman, Spaniard, or Greek, or anyone from southern Europe, just as a Dutchman means anyone from a Fin down to a real Hollander; so I wasn't much wiser. However, in a day or two Bill Walker came up to me and told me, in a confidential London twang, that he now believed Matthias, as he called himself, was a half-caste Malay, as I had thought at first. But I was to know him better afterward, as will be seen before I finish.

Now, it is a strange thing, and it shows how hard it is for a man not accustomed to writing, like myself, to tell a story in the proper way, that I have not said anything of the passengers who were going with us to San Francisco. I could understand it if I had been writing this down just at the time these things happened, but when I think that I have put the Malay before Elsie Fleming, even if he came into my life first, I am almost ready to laugh at my own stupidity. For Elsie was the brightest, bonniest girl I ever saw, and even now I find it hard not to let the cat out of the bag before the hour. As a matter of fact, this being the third time I have written all this over, I had to cut out pages about Elsie which did not come in their proper place. So now I shall say no more than that Elsie and her sister Fanny, and their father, took passage with us to California, as we were the only sailing vessel going that way; and old Fleming, who had been a sailor himself, fairly hated steamboats—aye, a good deal worse than I do, for I think them a curse to sailors. But when they came on board I was busy as a mate is when ready to go to sea, and though I believe I must have been blind, yet I hardly took any notice of the two sisters, more than to remark that one had hair like gold and a laugh which was as sweet as a fair wind up Channel. But I came to know her better since; though in a way different from the Malay.

When we had got our anchor on board, and were fairly out to sea, heading for Bass's Straits, I saw her and Helen talking together, and I think it was the contrast between the two that first attracted me toward her, not much liking dark women, being dark myself. She seemed, compared with Will's wife, as fair as an angel from heaven, though the glint of her eyes, and her quick, bright ways, showed she was a woman all over. I took a fancy to her that moment, and I believe Helen saw it, when I think over what has happened since, for she frowned and bit her lip hard, until I could see a mark there. But I didn't know then what I do now, and besides, I had no time to think about such things just then, for we were hard at it getting things shipshape.

Tom Mackenzie, the second officer, and a much older man than myself—for he had been to sea for seventeen years before he took it into his head to try for his second mate's ticket—came up to me when the men were mustered aft.

"Mr. Ticehurst," said he gruffly, "I should be glad if you'd take that Malay chap in your watch, for I have two d—d Dagos already, who are always quarreling, and if I have three, there will be bloodshed for sure. I don't like his looks."

"No more do I," I answered; "but I don't care for his looks. I've tamed worse looking men; and if you ask it, Mackenzie, why I'll have him and you can take the Cockney."

I think this was very good of me, for Bill Walker, I could see, was a real smart hand, and a merry fellow, not one of those grumblers who always make trouble for'ard, and come aft at the head of a deputation once a week growling about the victuals. But Mackenzie was a good sort, and though he was under me, I knew that for practical seamanship—though I won't take a back seat among any men of my years at sea—he was ahead of all of us. So I was ready to do him a good turn, and it was true enough he had two Greeks in his watch already.

When we had been to sea about a week, and got into the regular routine of work, which comes round just as it does in a house, for it is never done, Will got into his routine, too, and was drunk every day just as regular as eight bells at noon. Helen came to me, of course.

"Tom, can't you do something?" she said, with tears in her eyes, the first time I ever saw them there, though not the last. "It is horrible to think of his drinking this way! And then before those two girls—I am ashamed of myself and of him! Can't you do anything?"

"What can I do, Helen?" I asked. "I can't take it from him; I can't stave the liquor, there's too much of it; besides, he is captain, if he is my brother, and I can't go against him."

"But can't you try and persuade him, Tom?" and she caught my arm and looked at me so sorrowfully.

"Haven't I done it, Helen!" I answered. "Do you think I have seen him going to hell these two years without speaking? But what good is it—what good is it?"

She turned away and sat down by Elsie and Fanny, while just underneath in the saloon Will was singing some old song about "Pass the bottle round." He did, too, and it comes round quick at a party of one.

I can see easily that if I tell everything in this way I shall never finish my task until I have a pile of manuscript as big as the log of a three years' voyage, so I shall have to get on quickly, and just say what is necessary, and no more. And now I must say that by this time I was in love with Elsie Fleming, in love as much as a man can be, in love with a passion that trial only strengthened, and time could not and cannot destroy. It was no wonder I loved her, for she was the fairest, sweetest maid I ever saw, with long golden hair, bright blue eyes that looked straight at one, but which could be very soft too sometimes, and a neat little figure that made me feel, great strong brute that I was, as clumsy as an ox, though I was as quick yet to go aloft as any young man if occasion called for the mate to show his men the way. And when we were a little more than half across the Pacific to the Golden Gate, I began to think that Elsie liked me more than she did anyone else, for she would often talk to me about her past life in sunny New South Wales, and shiver to think that her father might insist on staying a long time in British Columbia, for he was going to take possession of a farm left him by an old uncle near a place called Thomson Forks.

It was sweet to have her near me in the first watch, and I cursed quietly to myself when young Jack Harmer, the apprentice, struck four bells, for at ten o'clock she always said, "Good-night, Mr. Ticehurst. I must go now. How sleepy one does get at sea! Dear me, how can you keep your eyes open?" And when she went down it seemed as if the moon and stars went out.

When it was old Mackenzie's first watch I was almost fool enough to be jealous of her being with him then, though he had a wife at home, and a daughter just as old as Elsie, and he thought no more of women, as a rule, than a hog does of harmony, as I once heard an American say. Still, when I lay awake and heard her step overhead, for I knew it well, I was almost ready to get up then and there and make an unutterable fool of myself by losing my natural sleep.

And now I am coming to what I would willingly leave out. I hope that people won't think badly of me for my share in it, for though I was not always such a straight walker in life as some are, yet I would not do what evil-minded folks might think I did. Somehow I have a difficulty in putting it down, for though I have spoken of it sometimes sorrowfully enough to one who is very dear to me, yet to write it coolly on paper seems cowardly and treacherous. And yet, seeing that I can harm no one, and knowing as I do in my heart that I wasn't to blame, I must do it, and do it as kindly as I can. This is what I mean: I began to see that Helen loved me more than she should have done, and that she hated Will bitterly, but Elsie even worse.

It was a great surprise to me, for, to tell the truth, women as a general rule have never taken to me very much, and Will was always the one in our family who had most to do with them. And for my part, until I saw Elsie I never really loved anyone, although, like most men, I have had a few troubles which until then I thought love-affairs. So it was very hard to convince myself that what I suspected was true, even though I believe that I have a natural fitness for judging people and seeing through them, even women, who some folks say do not act from reason like men. However, I don't think they are much different, for few of us act reasonably. But all this has nothing to do with the matter in hand. Now, I must confess, although it seems wicked, that I was a little pleased at first to think that two women loved me, for we are all vain, and that certainly touches a man's vanity, and yet I was sorry too, for I foresaw trouble unless I was very careful, though not all the woe and pain which came out of this business before the end.

The first thing that made me suspect something was wrong, was that Helen almost ceased to keep Will from the bottle, and she taunted him bitterly, so bitterly, that if he had not usually been a good-tempered fellow even when drunk, he might have turned nasty and struck her. And then she would never leave me and Elsie alone if she could help it, although she was not hypocrite enough to pretend to be very fond of her. Indeed, Elsie said one night to me that she was afraid Mrs. Ticehurst didn't like her. I laughed, but I saw it was true. Then, whenever she could, Helen came and walked with me, and she hardly ever spoke. It seems to me now, when I know all, that she was in a perpetual conflict, and was hardly in her right mind. I should like to think that she was not.

I was in a very difficult position, as any man will admit. I loved Elsie dearly; I was convinced my brother's wife loved me; and we were all four shut up on ship-board. I think if we had been on land I should have spoken to Elsie and run away from the others, but here I could not speak without telling her more than I desired, or without our being in the position of lovers, which might have caused trouble. For I even thought, so suspicious does a man get, that Helen might perhaps have come on board more on my account than on Will's.

All this time we were making very fair headway, for we had a good breeze astern of us, and the "Islands" (as they call them in San Francisco), that is the Sandwich Islands, were a long way behind us. If we had continued to have fine weather, or if Will had kept sober, or even so drunk that he could not have interfered in working the ship, things might not have taken the turn they did, and what happened between me and the Malay who called himself Matthias might never have occurred. And when I look back on the train of circumstances, it almost makes me believe in Fate, though I should be unwilling to do that; for I was taught by my mother, a very intelligent woman who read a great deal of theology, that men have free will and can do as they please.

However, when we were nearing the western coast of America, Will, who had a great notion—a much greater one than I had, by the way—of his navigation, began to come up every day and take his observations with me, until at last the weather altered so for the worse, and it came on to blow so hard, that neither of us could take any more. Now, if Will drank enough, Heaven knows, in fine weather, he drank a deal harder in foul, though by getting excited it didn't have the usual effect on him, and he kept about without going to sleep just where he sat or lay down. So he was always on deck, much to my annoyance, for I could see the men laughing as he clung to the rail at the break of the poop, bowing and scraping, like an intoxicated dancing master, with every roll the *Vancouver* made.

For five days we had been running by dead reckoning, and as well as I could make out we were heading straight for the coast, a good bit to the nor'ard of our true course. Besides, we were a good fifty miles farther east than Will made out, according to his figures, and I said as much to him. He laughed scornfully. "I'm captain of this ship," said he; "and Tom—don't you interfere. If I've a mind to knock Mendocino County into the middle of next week, I'll do it! But I haven't, and we are running just right."

You see, when he was in this state he was a very hard man to work with, and if we differed in our figures I had often enough a big job to convince him that he was wrong. And being wrong even a second in the longitude means being sixty miles out. And with only dead reckoning to rely on, we should have been feeling our way cautiously toward the coast, seeing that in any case we might fetch up on the Farallon Islands, which lie twenty miles west of the Golden Gate.

On the sixth day of this weather it began to clear up a little in the morning watch, and there seemed some possibility of our getting sight of the sun before eight bells. Will was on deck, and rather more sober than usual.

"Well, sir," said I to him, for I was just as respectful, I'll swear, as if he was no relation, "there seems a chance of getting an observation; shall we take it?"

"Very well," said he. "Send Harmer here, and we'll wait for a chance."

Harmer came aft, and brought up Will's sextant, and just then the port foretopsail sheet parted, for it was really blowing hard, though the sun came out at intervals. I ran forward myself, and by the time the watch had clewed up the sail and made it fast, eight bells had struck. When I went aft I met Harmer.

"Did you get an observation!" I asked anxiously, for when a man has the woman he loves on board it makes him feel worried, especially if things go as they were going then.

"Yes, Mr. Ticehurst," said he, "and the captain is working it out now. But, sir, if I were you I would go over it after him, for two heads are better than one," and he laughed, being a merry, thoughtless youngster, and went into his berth.

However, I did not do what he said, thinking that we should both get an observation at noon. We were very lucky to do so, for it began to thicken again at ten o'clock, and we were in a heavy fog until nearly twelve. And as soon as eight bells was struck, the fog which had lifted came down again.

When I got below Will already had the chart out, and was showing the women where we were, as he said; and when I came in he called me.

"There, look, Mr. Chief Officer! what did I tell you? Look!" and he pricked off our position as being just about where he had reckoned.

I took up the slate he had been making the calculation on, but he saw me, and snatched it out of my hand.

"What d'ye mean?" said he fiercely; "what do you want?" and he threw it on the deck, smashing it in four pieces. I made a sign to Elsie, and she picked them up like lightning, while Will called for the steward and some more brandy, and began drinking in a worse temper than I had ever seen him in.

When I passed Elsie she gave me the broken bits of slate, and I went into my cabin, pieced them together, and worked the whole thing out again. And when I had done it the blood ran to my head and I almost fell. For the morning observation which Will only had taken was wrongly worked out. I ran out on deck like lightning, and found it a thick fog all round us, for all the wind. Old Mackenzie was in the poop, and he roared out when he saw me:

"What's the matter, Tom Ticehurst?"

"Put the ship up into the wind, for God's sake!" I shouted. "And send a hand up aloft to look out, for the coast should be right under our bows. We must be in Ballinas Bay." And as he ported the helm, I rushed back into the cabin and took the chart out again to verify our position as near as I could. The coast ought to be in sight if the fog cleared. For we had run through or past the Farallones without seeing them.

When I came down the women all cried out at the sight of me, for though I controlled myself all I could, it was impossible, so sudden was the shock, to hide all I felt. And just then the *Vancouver* was coming into the wind, the men were at the lee braces, and as she dived suddenly into the head seas, her pitches were tremendous. It seemed to the women that something must be wrong, while Will, who, seaman-like, knew what had happened, though mad with drink, rushed on deck with a fierce oath. I dropped the chart and ran after him; yet I stayed a moment.

"It will be all right," I said to the women; "but I can't tell you now." And I followed Will, who had got hold of old Mackenzie by the throat, while the poor fellow looked thunderstruck.

"What the devil are you doing?" he screamed. "Why don't you keep the course? Man the weather-braces, you dogs, and put the helm up!"

But no one stirred; while Tom Mackenzie, seeing me there, took Will by the wrists and threw him away from him. I caught him as he fell, roaring, "Mutiny! Mutiny!"

"It's no mutiny!" I shouted, in my turn; "if we keep your course we shall be on the rocks in half an hour. I tell you the land is dead to loo-ard, aye, and not five miles off."

But it was less than that, for just then it cleared up a little. And the lookout on the foreyard shouted, "Land on the lee-bow!" Then he cried out, "Land right ahead!" Whether Will heard him or not, I don't know, but he broke away from me and fell, rather than went, down the companion, and in a moment I heard the women scream.

I caught Mackenzie by the arm.

"It's for our lives, and the lives of the women? He's gone for his revolver! I shall take command!"

And I sprang behind the companion like lightning. And just in time, for, as Will came up, I saw he was armed, and I jumped right on his back. His revolver went off and struck the taffrail; the next moment I had kicked it forward to where Mackenzie was standing, and grasped Will by the arms.

I had never given him credit for the strength he showed, but then he was mad, mad drunk, and it was not till Walker and Matthias—for all hands were on deck by this time—came to help me that I secured him. In the struggle Will drew back his foot and kicked the Malay in the face, and as he rose, with the evilest look I ever saw on a man's countenance, he drew his knife instinctively. With my left hand I caught his wrist and nearly broke it, while the knife flew out of his hand. And then, even by that simple action, I saw that I had made an enemy of this man, whom up to this time I had always been kind to and treated with far more consideration than he would have got from rough old Mac. But this is only by the way, though it is important enough to the story.

I had to tie Will's hands, and all the time he foamed at the mouth, ordering the crew to assist him.

"I'll have you hung, you dogs, all of you!" he shrieked, while the three women stood on the companion-ladder, white and trembling with fear.

It was with great trouble that we got him below, and when he was there I shut him in his berth, and sent the two stewards in with him to see that he neither did himself harm nor got free, and then I turned my attention to saving the ship and our lives.

We were in an awfully critical situation, and one which, in ordinary circumstances, might have made a man's heart quail; but now—with the woman I loved on board—it was maddening to think of, and made me curse my brother who had brought us into it. Think of what it was. Not five miles on our lee-bow there was the land, and we could even distinguish as we lifted on the sea the cruel line of white breakers which seemed to run nearly abeam, for the *Vancouver* was not a very weatherly ship, and the gale, instead of breaking, increased, until, if I had dared, I would have ordered sail to be shortened.

I went to the chart again. Just as I took it, Mackenzie called to me, "Mr. Ticehurst, there's a big flat-topped mountain some way inland. I think it must be Table Mountain." Yes, he knew the coast, and even as I looked at the chart, I heard him order the helm to be put up. I saw why, for when we had hauled into the wind, we were heading dead for the great four-fathom bank that lies off Bonita Point. But there was a channel between it and the land.

I ran on deck and spoke to Mackenzie. He pointed out on the starboard hand, and there the water was breaking on the bank. We were running for the narrow channel under a considerable press of canvas, seeing how it blew; for all Mac relieved her of when we first put her into the wind was the main top-gallant sail. And now I could do nothing for a moment but try to get sight of our landmarks, and keep sight of them, for the weather was still thick.

Fortunately, as it might have seemed for us, the chain-cables had already been ranged fore and aft on the deck, and I told Mackenzie to see them bent on to the anchors, and the stoppers made ready. Yet I knew that if we had to anchor, we were lost; in such a gale it could only postpone our fate, for they would come home or part to a dead certainty.

Mackenzie and I stood together on the poop watching anxiously for the right moment to haul our wind again.

"What do you think of it, Mr. Mackenzie?" I said, as I clung on to a weather backstay. "Where do you think we shall be in half an hour?"

"I don't think I shall ever see Whitechapel again, sir," he answered quietly, and I knew he was thinking of home, of his wife and his daughter. "She will go to leeward like a butter-cask in this sea; and now look at the land!" And he pointed toward the line of breakers on the land, which came nearer and nearer. We waited yet a few minutes, and then I looked at Mackenzie inquiringly. "Yes, I think so, sir," he said, and with my hand I motioned the men at the wheel to put the helm down again. As she came into the wind the upper foretopsail blew out of the boltropes, while the vessel struggled like a beaten hound that is being dragged to execution, and shivered from stem to stern. For the waves were running what landsmen call mountains high; she now shipped a sea every moment, which came in a flood over the fo'c'sle head; and pouring down through the scuttle, the cover of which had been washed overboard, it sent the men's chests adrift in the fo'c'sle and washed the blankets out of the lower bunks. And to windward the roar of the breakers on the bank was deafening. I went below just for a moment. I knew I had no right to go there, my place was on deck, but could not help myself. I must see Elsie once more before we died, for if the vessel struck, the first sea that washed over her might take me with it, and we should never see each other again on earth. But the two sisters were not in the saloon. I stepped toward their berth, and Helen met me, rising up from the deck, where she had been crouching down in terror.

I have said she was beautiful; and so she was when she smiled, and the pleasant light fell about her like sunlight on some strange and rare tropical flower, showing her rosy complexion, her delicate skin of full-blooded olive, and her coils of dark and shining hair But I never saw her so beautiful as she was then, clothed strangely with the fear of death, white with passion that might have made a weaker woman crimson with shame, and fiercely triumphant with a bitter self-conquest. She caught me by the arm. "Tom, dear Tom," she said, in a wonderful voice that came to me clearly through the howl of the wind, "I know there is not hope for us. He" (and she pointed toward her husband's cabin) "has ruined us! I hate him! And, Tom, now it is all over, and we shall not live! Say good-by to me, say good-by!"

I stood thunderstruck and motionless, for I knew what she meant even before she put up her hands and took me round the neck. "Kiss me once, just once, and I will die—for now I could not live, and would not! Kiss me!" And I did kiss her. Why, I know not, whether out of pity (it was not love—no, not love of any kind, I swear) or from the strong constraint of her force of mind, I cannot say; and as I lifted my head from hers, I saw Elsie, the woman I did love, looking at me with shame at my fall, as she thought, and with scorn. I freed myself from Helen, who sank down on her knees without seeing that she had been observed, and I went toward Elsie. She, too, was pale, though not with fear, for perhaps she was ignorant of her danger, but as I thought with a little feeling of triumph even then, for we are strange beings, with jealousy and anger.

"You are a coward and a traitor!" she said, when I reached her.

"No, no, I am not, Elsie," I answered sharply; "but perhaps you will never know that I am speaking the truth. But let that be; are you a brave woman? For—— But where is your father?"

"With Fanny," she answered, disdainfully even then.

I called him, and he came out.

"Mr. Fleming," I said; "you know our position; in a few minutes we shall be safe or—ashore. Get your daughters dressed warmly; stay at the foot of the companion with them, and, if it is necessary, come up when I call you."

The old man shook hands with me and pointed to Will's wife. I had forgotten her!

"Look after her, too," I said, and went to Will's cabin. He was fast asleep and snoring hard. I could hardly keep from striking him, but I let him lie. Was it a wonder that a woman ceased to love him? And I went on deck.

I had not been absent five minutes, but in that time the wind had increased even more, the seas seemed to have grown heavier, the decks were full of water, and the fatal wake was yet broader on the weather-quarter. All the men were aft under the break of the poop, and most of them, thinking that we must go ashore, had taken off their oilskins and sea-boots ready for an effort to save themselves at the last. Even in the state of mind that I was in then, I saw clearly, and the strange picture they presented—wet through, some with no hats on, up to their knees in water, for the decks could not clear themselves, though some of the main deck ports were stove in and some out in the bulwarks—remains vividly with me now. Among them stood Matthias, with a red handkerchief over his head, and a swelled cheek, where Will had struck him. By his side was Walker, the only man in the crowd who seemed cheerful, and he actually smiled. Perhaps he was what the Scotch called "fey."

Suddenly Mackenzie called me loudly.

"Look sir, look! There is the point, the last of the land! It's Bonita Point, if I know this coast at all!"

I sprang into the weather mizzen rigging, and the men, who had noticed the second mate's gestures, did the same at the main. I could see the Point, and knew it, and I knew if we could only weather it we could put the helm up and run into San Francisco in safety. Just then Harmer, who was as cool as a cucumber, struck four bells, and Matthias and a man called Thompson, an old one-eyed sailor, came up to relieve the wheel.

The point which we had to weather was about as far from us as the land dead to leeward, and it was touch and go whether we should clear it or not. The *Vancouver* made such leeway, closehauled, that it seemed doubtful, and I fancied we should have a better chance if I freed her a little, to let her go through the water faster. Yet it was a ticklish point, and one not to be decided without thought in a situation which demanded instant action.

"What think you, Mac," said I hurriedly; "shall we ease her half a point?"

He nodded, and I spoke to the men at the wheel, and as I did so I noticed the Malay's face, which was ghastly with fear, although he seemed steady enough. But I thought it best to alter the way they stood, for the Englishman had the lee wheel. I ordered them to change places.

"What's that for, sir?" said Matthias, almost disrespectfully. I stared at him.

"Do as you are told, you dog!" I answered roughly, for I had no time to be polite. "I don't like your steering. I have noticed it before."

When the course was altered she got much more way on her, but neared the land yet more rapidly. I called the men on to the poop, for I had long before this determined not to chance the anchors, and looked down into the saloon to see if the women were there.

As I did so Mr. Fleming called me.

"If I can be of any use, Mr. Ticehurst, I am ready."

"I think not, Mr. Fleming," I replied as cheerfully as possible; "we shall be out of danger in a few minutes—or on the rocks," I added to myself, as I closed the hatch.

It was a breathless and awful time, and I confess that for a few moments I forgot the very existence of Elsie, as I calculated over and over again the chances as we neared the Point. It depended on a hair, and when I looked at Mackenzie, who was silent and gloomy, I feared the worst. Yet it shows how strangely one can be affected by one's fellows that when I saw Harmer and Walker standing side by side their almost cheerful faces made me hope, and I smiled. But we were within three cables' length of the Point, and the roar of the breakers came up against the wind until it deafened us. I watched the men at the wheel, and I saw Matthias flinch visibly as though he had been struck by a whip. I didn't know why it was, I am not good at such things, but I took a deeper dislike to him that moment than I had ever had, and I stepped up to him. Now in what followed perhaps I myself was to blame, and yet I feel I could not have acted differently. Perhaps I looked threatening at him as I approached, but at any rate he let go the wheel and fell back on the gratings. With an angry oath I jumped into his place, struck him with my heel, and then I saw Walker make a tremendous spring for me, with an expression of alarm in his face, as he looked beyond me, that made me make a half turn. And that movement saved my life. I felt the knife of Matthias enter my shoulder like a red-hot iron, and then it was wrenched out of his hand and out of the wound by Walker.

In a moment the two were locked together, and in another they were separated by Mackenzie and the others; and Walker stood smiling with the knife in his hand. Although the blood was running down my body, I did not feel faint, and kept my eye fixed on the course kept by the *Vancouver*, while Mackenzie held me in his arms, and Harmer took the lee wheel from me.

"Luff a little!" I cried, for we were almost on the Point, and I saw a rock nearly dead ahead. "Luff a little!" and they put the helm down on a spoke or two.

The moments crawled by, and the coast crawled nearer and nearer, as I began to feel I was going blind and fainting. But I clung to life and vision desperately, and the last I saw was what I can see now, and shall always see as plainly, the high black Point with its ring of white water crawl aft and yet nearer, aft to the foremast, aft to the mainmast and then I fell and knew no more. For we were saved.

When I came to, we were before the wind, and I lay on a mattress in the cabin. Near me was Elsie, and by her Helen, who was as white as death. Both were watching me, and when I opened my eyes Helen fell on her knees and suddenly went crimson, and then white again, and fainted. But Elsie looked harder and sterner than I had ever seen her. I turned my face away, and near me I saw another mattress with a covered figure on it, the figure of a dead man, for I knew the shape. In my state of faintness a strange and horrible delirium took possession of me. It seemed as if what I saw was seen only by myself, and that it was a prophecy of my death. I fainted again.

When I came to we were at anchor in San Francisco Bay, and a doctor from the shore was attending to me, while Mackenzie stood by, smiling and rubbing his hands as if delighted to get me off them. I looked at him and he knelt down by me.

"Mackenzie, old man," I whispered, "didn't I see somebody dead here?"

"Aye, poor chap," he answered, brushing away a tear; "it was poor Walker."

"Walker!" I said. "How was that?"

"Accident, sir," said old Mac. "Just as we rounded the Point and you fainted, the old bark gave a heavy roll as we put her before the wind, and Walker, as he was standing with that black dog's knife in his hand, slipped and fell. The blade entered his body, and all he said after was, 'It was his knife after all. He threatened to do for me yesterday.'"

"Where's Will?" I asked, when he ended, for I was somehow anxious to save my brother's credit, and I shouldn't have liked to see him dismissed from the ship.

"He's on deck now, as busy as the devil in a gale of wind," growled Mackenzie. "'Tis he that saved the ship. Oh, he's a mighty man!—but I don't sail with him no more."

However, he altered his mind about that.

Now, it has taken me a long time to get to this point, and perhaps if I had been a better navigator in the waters of story-telling I might have done just what Will didn't do, and have missed all the trouble of beating to windward to get round to this part of my story. I might have put it all in a few words, perhaps, but then I like people to understand what I am about, and it seems to me necessary. If it isn't, I dare say someone will tell me one of these days. At any rate, here I have got into San Francisco, a city I don't like by the way, for it is a rascally place, managed by the professional politicians, who are the worst men in it; I had been badly wounded, and the Malay was in prison, and (not having money) he was likely to stay there.

I was in the hospital for three weeks, and I never had a more miserable or lonely time. If I had not been stronger in constitution than most men I think I should have died, so much was I worried by my love for Elsie, who was going away thinking me a scoundrel, who had tried to gain the love of my brother's wife. Of course she did not come near me, though I knew the Flemings were still in the city. I learnt so much from Will, who had the grace to come and see me, thanking me, too, for having saved the *Vancouver.*

"You must get well soon, Tom," said he, "for I need you very much just now."

I kept silence, and he looked at me inquiringly.

"Will," I said at length, "I shall never I sail with you again—I can't do it."

"Why not?" he cried, in a loud voice, which made the nurse come up and request him to speak in a little lower tone. "Why not? I can't see what difference it will make, anything that has occurred."

No, he did not see, but then he did not know. How could I go in the ship again with Helen? Besides, I had determined to win Elsie for my wife, and how could I do that if I let her go now, thinking what she did of me?

"Well, Will, I can't go," said I once more; "and I don't think I shall go to sea again, I am sick of it."

Will stared, and whistled, and laughed.

"Ho!" said he; "I think I see how the land lies. You are going to settle in British Columbia, eh? You are a sly dog, but I can see through you. I know your little love-affair; Helen told me as much as that one day."

"Well, then, Will," I answered wearily, for I was out of heart lying there, "if you know, you can understand now why I am not going to sail with you. But, Will," and I rose on my elbow, hurting myself considerably as I did so, "let me implore you not to drink in future. Have done with it. It will be your ruin and your wife's—aye, and if I sailed with you, mine as well. Give me your hand, and say you will be a sober man for the future, and then I shall be content to go where I must go—aye, and where I will go."

He gave me his hand, that was hot with what he had been drinking even then (it was eleven in the morning), and I saw tears in his eyes.

"I will try, Tom," he muttered; "but——"

I think that "but" was the saddest word, and the most prophetic, I ever heard on any man's lips. I saw how vain it was, and turned away. He shook hands, and went without saying more than "Good-by, Tom." I saw him twice after that, and just twice.

By the time I was out of the hospital the *Vancouver* was ready to go to sea, being bound to England; and she might have sailed even then, only it was necessary for Tom Mackenzie and one or two others to remain as witnesses when they tried Matthias for stabbing me. I shall not go into a long description of the trial, for I have read in books of late so many trial scenes that I fear I should not have the patience to give details, which, after all, are not necessary, since the whole affair was so simple. And yet, what followed afterward from that affair I can remember as brightly and distinctly as if in a glass—the look of the dingy court, the fierce and revengeful eyes of Matthias, who never spoke till the last, and the appearance of Helen and Fanny (Elsie was not there)—when the judge after the verdict inflicted a sentence of eighteen months' hard labor on the prisoner. Perhaps he had been in prison before, and knew what it meant, or it was simply the bitter thought of a revengeful Oriental at being worsted by his opponent; but when he heard the sentence, he leant forward and grasped the rail in front of him tightly, and spoke. His skin was dark and yet pallid, the perspiration stood in beads on his forehead, he bit his lips until blood came, while his eyes looked more like the eyes of a human beast than those of a man. This is what he said as he looked at me, and he spoke with a strange intensity which hushed all noise.

"When I come out of jail I will track you night and day, wherever you go or whatever you do to escape me. Though you think I do not know where you are, I shall always be seeking for you, and at last I shall find you. If a curse of mine could touch you, you should rot and wither now, but the time will come when my hand shall strike you down!"

Such was the meaning of what he said, although it was not put exactly as I have here written it down; and if I confess, as I should have to do at last before the end of this story comes, that the words and the way they were spoken—spoken so vehemently and with so fixed a resolution—made me shiver and feel afraid in a way I had never done before, I hope nobody will blame me; but I am sure that being in love makes a coward of a man in many ways, and in one moment I saw myself robbed of life and love just at their fruition. I beheld myself clasping Elsie to my bosom, having won from her at last an avowal of her love, and then stabbed or shot in her arms. Ah! it was dreadful the number of fashions my mind went to work, in a quick fever of black apprehension, to foretell or foresee my own possible doom. I had never thought myself cowardly, but then I seemed to see what death meant better than I had ever done; and often the coward is what he is, as I think now, from a vivid imagination, which so many of us lack. I went out of the court in a strange whirl, for you see I had only just recovered. If I had been quite well I might have laughed instead of feeling as I did. But I did not laugh then.

Now, on the next morning the *Vancouver* was to leave the harbor, being then at anchor off Goat Island. All the money that was due to me I had taken, for Will had given me my discharge, and I sent home for what I had saved, being quite uncertain what I should do if I followed Elsie to British Columbia. And that night I saw the last of Will, the last I ever saw, little thinking then how his fate and mine were bound up together, nor what it was to be. Helen was with him, and I think if he had been sober or even gentle with her in his drink, she would have never spoken to me again as she did on that day when she believed that life was nearly at its end for both of us. But Will, having finished all his business, had begun to drink again, and was in a vile temper as we sat in a room at the American Exchange Hotel, where I was staying. Helen tried to prevent his drinking.

"Will," she said, in rather a hard voice from the constraint she put on herself, "you have had enough of drink, we had better go on board."

"Go on board yourself," said he, "and don't jaw me! I wish I had left you in Australia. A woman on board a ship is like a piano in the fo'c'sle. Come and have a drink, Tom."

"No, thank you," I said; "I have had quite enough."

And out he went, standing drinks at the bar to half a dozen, some of whom would have cut his throat for a dollar, I dare say, by the looks of them. Then Helen came over and sat down by me.

"I have never spoken to you, Tom," she began, and then she stopped, "since—you know, since that dreadful day outside there," and she pointed, just like a woman who never knows the bearings of a place until she has reckoned out how the house points first, to the East when she meant the West, "and now I feel I must, because I may never have the chance again."

She took out her handkerchief, although she was dry-eyed, and twisted it into a regular ground-swell knot, until I saw the stuff give way here and there. She seemed unable to go on, and perhaps she would not have said more if we hadn't heard Will's voice, thick with drink, as he demanded more liquor.

"Hear him!" she said hurriedly, "hear the man who is my husband! What a fool I was! You don't know, but I was. And I am his wife! Ah! I could kill him! I could! I could!"

I was horrified to see the passion she was in; it seemed to have a touch of real male fury in it, just as when a man is trying to control himself, feeling that if one more provocation is given him he will commit murder, for she shook and shivered, and her voice was strangely altered.

And just then Will came back, demanding with an oath if she was ready to go. She never spoke, but I should have been sorry to have any woman look at me as she did at him when his eyes were off her. I shook hands with her and with him, for the last time, and they went away.

Next morning, being lonely and having nothing to do I went out to the park, made on the great sand-dunes which runs from the higher city to the ocean beach and the Cliff House on the south side of the Golden Gate. For the sake of a quiet think I went out by the cars, and walked to a place where few ever came but chance visitors, except on Sunday. It is just at the bend of the great drive and a little above the road, where there is a large tank with a wooden top, which makes a good seat from which one can see back to San Francisco and across the bay to Oakland, Saucelito, and the other little watering-places in the bay; or before one, toward the opening of the Golden Gate, and the guns of Alcatraz Island, where the military prison is. Here I took my seat and looked out on the quiet beautiful bay and the sea just breaking in a line of foam on the beach beneath me. The sight of the ships at anchor was rather melancholy to me, for my life had been on the sea. It seemed as if a new and unknown life were before me; and a sailor starting anything ashore is as strange as though some inveterate dweller in a city should go to sea. There were one or two white sails outside the Heads, and one vessel was being towed in; there was a broad wake from the Saucelito ferry-boat, and far out to sea I saw the low Farallones lying like a cloud on the horizon. It was beyond them that my new life had begun, really begun; and though the day was fair, I knew not how soon foul weather might overtake me, and I knew indeed that it could only be postponed unless fate were very kind. I don't know how long I sat on that tank drumming on the hollow wood, as I idly picked up the pebbles from the ground and threw them down into the road; but at last I saw what I had partly been waiting for—the *Vancouver* being towed out to sea. I had no need to look at her twice; I knew every rope in her, and every patch of paint, to say nothing of her masts being ranked a little more than is usual nowadays. I had no glass with me, but I fancied I could see a patch of color on her poop that was Helen.

I watched the vessel which had been my home—and which, but for me, would have been lying a wreck over yonder—for more than an hour, and then I turned to go home, if I can call an American hotel "home" by strained politeness, and just then I saw a carriage come along. Now, I knew as well before I could distinguish them that Elsie, Fanny, and her father were in that carriage, as I did that Helen was on board the *Vancouver*; and I sat down again feeling very faint—I suppose from the effects of my wound, or the illness that came from it. The carriage had almost passed beneath me—and I felt Elsie saw me, though she made no sign—before Mr. Fleming caught sight of me.

"Hi! stop!" he called, and the driver drew up. "Why, Mr. Ticehurst, is that you? I thought the *Vancouver* had gone? Besides, how does a mate find time to be out here? Things must have changed since I was at sea. Come down! Come down!"

I did so, and shook hands with them all, though Elsie's hand lay in mine like a dead thing until she drew it away.

"The *Vancouver* has gone, Mr. Fleming," said I; "and there she is—look!"

They all turned, and Elsie kept her eyes fixed on it when the others looked at me again.

"Well," said Fleming, "what does it all mean? Where are you going? Back to town? That's right, get in!" And without more ado the old man, who had the grip of a vise, caught hold of me, and in I came like a bale of cotton. "Drive on!"

"Now then," he went on, "you can tell us why you didn't go with them."

I paused a minute, watching Elsie.

"Well, Mr. Fleming," I said at last, "you see I didn't quite agree with my brother."

"H'm!—calls taking the command from the captain not quite agreeing with him," chuckled Fleming; "but I thought you made it up, didn't you?"

"Yes, we made it up, but I wouldn't sail with him any more. I had more than one reason."

Again I looked at Elsie, and she was, I thought, a little pleasanter, though she did not speak. But Fanny pinched her arm, I could see that, and looked roguishly at me. However, Mr. Fleming, did not notice that byplay.

"Well," he said, a trifle drily as I fancied, "I won't put you through your catechism, except to ask you in a fatherly kind of way" (Elsie looked down and frowned) "what you are going to do now. I should have thought after what that rascal of a half-bred Malay, or whatever he is, said, that you would have left California in a hurry."

"Time enough, Mr. Fleming—time enough. I have eighteen months to look out on without fear of a knife in my ribs, and I may be in China, or Alaska, or the Rocky Mountains then."

You see I wanted to give them a hint that I might turn up in British Columbia. Fanny gave me a better chance though, and I could have hugged her for it.

"Or British Columbia perhaps, Mr. Ticehurst?" she said smiling very innocently.

"Who knows," I answered, hastily; "when a man begins to travel, there is no knowing where he may turn up. I had a fancy to go to Alaska, though."

For the way to Alaska was the way to British Columbia, and I did not want to surprise them too much if I went on the same steamer as far as Victoria. And in four days I might see what chance I really had with Elsie.

"Well," said the father, thoughtfully, "I don't know, and can't give advice. I should have thought that when a man was a good sailor and held your position he ought to stick to it. A rolling stone gathers no moss."

"Yes," I answered, "but I am tired of the sea."

"So am I," said Fanny, "and I don't blame you, though you ought to go with careless captains just on purpose to save people's lives, you know, Mr. Ticehurst; for you saved ours, and I think some of us might thank you better than by sitting like a dry stick without saying a word."

With this she dug at Elsie with her elbow, smiling sweetly all the time.

"Yes," said Elsie, "and there is Mr. Harmer now in the *Vancouver*. Perhaps she will be wrecked."

This was the first word she had spoken since I had entered the carriage, and I recognized by its spite that Elsie was a woman not above having a little revenge. For poor Fanny, who had flirted quite a little with Harmer, said no more.

They put down at their hotel, and I went inside with them.

"Well," said Fleming, "I suppose we shan't see you again, unless you do as Fanny says, and turn up in our new country. If you do, be sure we shall welcome you. And I wish you well, my boy."

I shook hands with them again, and turned away; and as I did so, I noticed some of their boxes marked, "Per SS. *Mexico*." Fanny saw me looking, and whispered quickly, as she passed me, "Tom Ticehurst, go to Mexico!" and vanished, while Elsie stood in the gaslight for a moment as if in indecision. But she turned away.

PART II. SAN FRANCISCO AND NORTHWARD.

I never felt so miserable and so inclined to go to sea to forget myself in hard work as I did that evening after I had bidden farewell to Elsie and her people. It seemed to me that she had let me go too easily out of her life for her to really care for me enough to make her influence my course in the way I had hoped, and hoped still. Indeed, I think that if she had not stayed that one undecided moment after she withdrew her hand from mine, I should have never done what I did do, but have looked for a ship at once. For, after all, I said to myself, what could a modest girl do more? Why, under the circumstances, when she thought me guilty of a deliberate crime, hateful to any woman, to say nothing of my having made love to her at the same time, it was really more than I could have expected or hoped. It showed that I had a hold upon her affections; and then Fanny thought so too, or she would have never said what she did. "Go to Mexico!" indeed; if I wasn't a fool, it was not Mexico the country, but *Mexico* the steamer she meant. I had one ally, at any rate. Still, I wondered if she knew what Elsie did, though I thought not, for she alone kissed Helen when they said good-by, and Elsie had only given her her hand unwillingly. If I could speak to Fanny it might help me. But I was determined to go northward, and sent my dunnage down on board the steamer that very evening.

In the morning, and early, for I lay awake all that night, a thing I did not remember having done before, I went down on the Front at the bottom of Market Street, where all the tram cars start, and walked to and fro for some hours along the wharves where they discharge lumber, or ship the coal. It was quite a bright morning in the late autumn, and everything was pleasant to look upon in the pure air before it was fouled by the oaths of the drivers of wagons and the jar of traffic. Yet that same noise, which came dimly to me until I was almost run over by a loaded wagon, pleased me a great deal better than the earlier quiet of the morning, and by eight o'clock I was in a healthy frame of mind, healthy enough to help three men with a heavy piece of lumber just by way of exercise. I went back to my room, washed my hands, had breakfast, and went on board the steamer, careless if the Flemings saw me, though at first I had determined to keep out of their way until the vessel was at sea. I thanked my stars that I did so, for I saw Fanny by herself on deck, and when she caught sight of me she clapped her hands and smiled.

"Well, and where are you going, Mr. Ticehurst?" said she, nodding at me as if she guessed my secret.

"I am going to take your advice and go to Mexico!" I answered.

"Is it far here? By land do you go, or water?"

"Not far, Fanny; in fact——"

"You are——"

"There now!" said I, laughing in my turn.

"Oh, I am so glad, Mr. Ticehurst!" said she; "for——" and then she stopped.

"For what, Fanny?" I asked.

"I'm afraid I can't tell you. I should be a traitor, and that is cowardly."

"No, Fanny, not when we are friends. If you tell me, would you do any harm?"

"No," she answered doubtfully.

"Then treachery is meant to do harm, and if you don't mean harm it isn't treachery," I replied coaxingly, but with bad logic as I have been told since.

"Well, then, perhaps I'll say something. Now suppose you liked me very much——"

"So I do, Fanny, I swear!"

"No you don't, stupid! How can you? I'm not twins—that is, I and somebody else aren't the same—so don't interrupt. Suppose you liked me very much, and I liked you very much——"

"It would be very nice, I dare say," I said, in a doubtful way that was neither diplomatic nor complimentary.

"And suppose you went off, and suppose I didn't speak to my sister for hours, and kept on being a nasty thing by tossing and tumbling about all night, so that she, poor girl, couldn't go to sleep; and then suppose when she did go off nicely, she woke up to find me—what do you think—crying, what would it mean?"

"Fanny," I exclaimed, in delight, "you are a dear girl, the very dearest——"

"No," she said, "no!"

"That I ever saw. If there weren't so many folks about, I would kiss you!"

And I meant it, but Fanny burst into laughter.

"The idea! I should like to see you try it. I would box your ears till they were as red as beetroot. But there, Tom, I am glad you are coming on this dirty steamer. For I have no one to talk to now but Elsie, and she won't talk at all."

However, Fanny's little woes did not trouble me much, for I was thinking of my own, and wondering how I ought to act.

"Fanny," said I, "tell me what I shall do. Shall I lie low and not show up until we are out at sea, or what?"

"If you don't want them to see you, you had better look sharp, for they are coming up now, I see Elsie's hat," said Fanny. And I dived out of sight round the deck house, and by dint of skillful navigation I got into my bunk without any one seeing me.

Now, the way Elsie found out I was on board was very curious, and perhaps more pleasing to Fanny than to her. My bunk was an upper one, and through the open porthole I could look out on to the wharf. As I lay there, in a much happier frame of mind than I had known for many days, I stared out carelessly, watching the men at work, and the passers-by; and suddenly to my great astonishment, I saw young Harmer looking very miserable and unhappy. He had left the *Vancouver*, too, but of course without leave, as he was an apprentice. Now, if I was surprised I was angry, too. It was such a foolish trick, and I thought I would give him a talking to at once. I spoke through the port.

"You infernal young fool!" said I, "what are you doing here? Why did you leave your ship?"

If ever I saw a bewildered face it was Harmer's. For some seconds he looked everywhere for the voice, and could not locate it either on the wharf, deck, or anywhere else.

"You ought to be rope's-ended for an idiot!" I went on, and then he saw part of my face, but without knowing who I was. He flushed crimson, and looked like a young turkeycock, with his wings down and his tail up.

"Who the devil are you, anyhow," he asked fiercely. "You come out here and I'll pull your ugly head off!"

"Thank you," I answered calmly, "my head is of more use to me than yours is, apparently; and if you don't know my voice, it belongs to Tom Ticehurst!"

Harmer jumped.

"Hurrah! Oh, I'm so glad. I was looking for you, Mr. Ticehurst, and hunting everywhere."

"And not for anyone else, I suppose?" I put in, and then I saw him look up. I knew just as well as he did that he saw Fanny, and I hoped that Elsie was not with her. But she was.

"How d'ye do, Miss Fleming?" said he nervously; "and you, Miss Fanny? I hope you are well. I was just talking to Mr. Ticehurst."

I swore a little at this, and tumbled out of my bunk, and went on deck to face the music, as the Americans say, and I got behind the girls in time to hear the little hypocrite Fanny say sweetly:

"Oh, Mr. Harmer, you must be mistaken, I'm sure! Mr. Ticehurst if going to Mexico or somewhere. He can't be here."

"Miss Fanny," said the boy earnestly, "I tell you he is, and there—just behind you. By Jove, I am coming on board!"

And he scrambled up the side like a monkey, as Elsie turned and saw me.

I said good-morning to her and we shook hands. I could see she was nervous, and fancied I could see traces of what Fanny, who talked hard, had told me.

"Dear me, Mr. Ticehurst!" said Fanny vigorously. "You didn't shake hands with me, and see the time it is since we last met! Why, was it yesterday, or when? But men are so forgetful. I never did like boys when I was a little girl, and I shall keep it up. Yes, Mr. Harmer, now I can shake hands, for not having arms ten feet long I couldn't reach yours over the rail, though you did hold them out like a signal post."

Then she and Harmer talked, and I lost what they said.

"Where is your father, Miss Fleming?" I asked, for though I felt obliged to talk, I could say nothing but that unless I remarked it was a fine day. But it had been fine for six months in California.

"He went ashore, Mr. Ticehurst, and won't be back until the steamer is nearly ready to go. But now I must go down. Come, Fanny!"

"What for?" demanded that young lady. "I'm not coming, I shall stay; I like the deck, and hate the cabin—misty stuffy hole! I shall not go down; as the pilot told the man in the stupid song: 'I shall pace the deck with thee,' Mr. Ticehurst, please."

"Thank you, Fanny," said I; "but I want to talk to Harmer here before the steamer goes, and if you will go with your sister perhaps it will be best."

She pouted and looked about her, and with a parting smile for Harmer, and a mouth for me, she followed Elsie. I turned to the lad.

"Now," I began, "you're a nice boy! What does it all mean?"

"It means that I couldn't stay on the *Vancouver* if you weren't there, Mr. Ticehurst. I made up my mind to that the moment I heard you were leaving. I will go on your next ship; but you know, if you don't mind my saying it, I couldn't stand your brother; I would rather be struck by you than called a cub by him. A 'cub,' indeed—I am as big as he is, and bigger!"

So he was, and a fine handsome lad into the bargain, with curly brown hair, though his features were a little too feminine for his size and strength.

"Harmer," I said drily "I think you have done it now very completely. This is my next ship, and I am a passenger in her."

He didn't seem to mind; in fact, he took it so coolly that I began to think he knew.

"That doesn't matter, Mr. Ticehurst," he said cheerfully; "I will come with you."

I stared.

"The devil you will! Do you know where I am going, what I am going to do?—or have you any plans of your own cut and dried for me?"

"I don't see that it matters, Mr. Ticehurst," he answered, with a coolness I admired; "I have more than enough to pay my fare, and if you go to British Columbia I dare say I can get something to do there."

"Ah? I see," I replied; "you are tired of the sea, and would like to marry and settle down, eh?"

He looked at me, and blushed a little.

"All the more reason I should go with you, sir; for then—then—there would be—you know."

"What, Harmer?" I asked.

"A pair of us," he answered humbly.

"H'm, you are a nice boy? What will your father say if he hears you have gone off in this way?"

Harmer looked at me and laughed.

"He will say it was your fault, sir! But I had better get my dunnage on board."

And away he went.

"Harmer, come back!" I cried, but he only turned, nodded cheerfully, and disappeared in the crowd.

On the whole, although the appearance of Harmer added a new responsibility to those which were already a sufficient burden, I was not ill-pleased, for I thoroughly liked him, and had parted with him very unwillingly when I shook his hand on board the *Vancouver* for the last time, as I thought then. At any rate, he would be a companion for me, and if by having to look after him I was prevented in any measure from becoming selfish about Elsie, I might thank his boyish foolishness in being unable to prevent himself running after Fanny, whom, to say the truth, I considered a little flirt, though a dear little girl. And, then, Harmer might be able to help me with Elsie. It was something to have somebody about that I could trust in case of accident.

It was nearer eleven than ten when the steamer's whistle shrieked for the last time, and the crew began to haul the warps on board. I could see that Elsie and Fanny were beginning to think that their father would arrive too late, when I saw him coming along the wharf with Harmer just behind him. Up to this time I really believed Mr. Fleming, with the curious innocence that fathers often show, even those who from their antecedents and character might be expected to know better, had never thought of me as being his daughter's lover; but when he had joined his daughters on the hurricane deck, and caught sight of Harmer and myself standing on the main, I saw in a moment that he knew almost as much as we could tell him, and that for a few seconds he was doubtful whether to laugh or to be angry. I saw him look at me sternly for a few seconds, then he shook his head with a very mixed smile on his weather-beaten face, and, sitting down on the nearest beach, he burst into laughter. I went up the poop ladder and caught Fanny's words:

"Why, father, what is the matter with you? Don't laugh so, all the people will think you crazy?"

"So I am, my dear, clean crazy," he answered; "because I fancied I saw Tom Ticehurst and young Harmer down on deck there, and of course it is impossible, I know that—quite impossible. It was an hallucination. For what could they want here, I should like to know? You don't know, of course? Well, well, I am surprised!"

Just then I came up and showed myself, looking quite easy, though I confess to feeling more like a fool than I remember doing since I was a boy.

"Oh, then you are here, Ticehurst?" said the old man. "It wasn't a vision, after all. I was just telling Fanny here that I thought I was going off my head."

I laughed.

"Why, Mr. Fleming," I said, "is it impossible that I, too, should go to Victoria, on my way to Alaska?"

Fleming looked at me curiously, and almost winked. "Ah! Alaska, to be sure," said he. "You did speak of Alaska. It must be a nice place. You will be quite close to us. Come over and give us a call."

"Thank you for the invitation," I replied, laughing. "I will come to tea, and bring my young friend with me."

For Harmer now walked up, shook hands with the old man in the most ordinary way, and sat down between him and Fanny with a coolness I could not have imitated for my life. It is a strange thing to think of the amount of impudence boys have from seventeen to twenty-three or so; they will do things a man of thirty would almost faint to attempt, and succeed because they don't know the risk they run. Harmer was soon engaged in talk with Fanny, and I tried in vain to imitate him. I found Elsie as cold as ice; I could make no impression on her and was almost in despair at the very outset. If Fanny had told me the truth in the morning, then Elsie held a great command over herself. I soon gave up the attack and retreated to my berth, where I smoked savagely and was miserable. You can see I did not understand much about women then.

The passage from San Francisco to Victoria takes about four days, and in that time I had to make up my mind what I was going to do. If what Fanny said were true, Elsie loved me, and it was only that foolish and wretched affair with Helen that stood in my way. Yet, could I tell the girl how matters were? It seemed to me then, and seems to me now, that I was bound in honor not to tell her. I could not say to her brutally that my brother's wife had made love to me, and that I was wholly blameless. It would be cowardly, and yet I ought to clear myself. It was an awkward dilemma. Then, again, it was quite possible that Fanny was mistaken; if she did not care for me, it was all the harder, and I could not court her with that mark against me. Yet I was determined to win her, and as I sat in my berth I grew fierce and savage in my heart. I swore that I would gain her over, I would force her to love me, if I had to kill any who stood in my way. For love makes a man devilish sometimes as well as good. I had come on board saying, "If I see no chance to win her before I get to Victoria, I will let her go." And now when we were just outside the Golden Gate, I swore to follow her always. "Yes, even if she spurns me, if she mocks, taunts me, I will make her come to me at last, put her arms round my neck, and ask my forgiveness." I said this, and unconsciously I added, "I will follow her night and day, in sunshine and in rain, in health or sickness."

Then I started violently, for I was using words like those of the Malay, who was waiting his time to follow me, and for ever in the daytime or nighttime I knew he was whetting the keen edge of his hate. I could see him in his cell; I could imagine him recalling my face to mind, for I knew what such men are. I had served as second mate in a vessel that had been manned with Orientals and the off-scourings of Singapore, such as Matthias was, and I knew them only too well. He would follow me, even as I followed her, and as she was a light before me, he would be a dark shadow behind me. I wished then that I had killed him on board the *Vancouver*, for I felt that we should one day meet; and who could discern what our meeting would bring forth in our lives? I know that from that time forward he never left me, for in the hour that I vowed to follow Elsie until she loved me, I saw very clearly that he would keep his word, though he had but strength to crawl after me and kill me as I slept. Henceforth, he was always more or less in my mind. Yet, if I could win Elsie first, I did not care. It might be a race between us, and her love might be a shield to protect me in my hour of need. I prayed that it might be so, and if it could not, then at least let me win her love before the end.

For two days I kept out of the Flemings' way, or rather out of the way of the girls, for Mr. Fleming himself could not be avoided, as he slept in the men's berth in a bunk close to mine. I believe that the first day on board he spoke to Elsie about me; indeed I know he did, for I heard so afterward; and I think it was only on her assurance that there was and could be nothing between us, that he endured the situation so easily. In the first place, although he was not rich, he was fairly well off in Australia; and though the British Columbian ranch property was not equal in value to that which he had made for himself, yet it represented a sum of money such as I could not scarcely make in many years in these hard times. It would hardly be human nature for a father to look upon me as the right sort of man for his daughter, especially since I was such a fool as to quit the sea without anything definite awaiting me on land. So, I say, that if he had thought that Elsie loved me I might have found him a disagreeable companion, and it was no consolation to me to see that he treated me in a sort of half-contemptuous, half-pitying way, for I would rather have seen him like one of the lizards on the Australian plains, such as the girls had told me of, which erect a spiny frill over their heads, and swell themselves out the whole length of their body until their natural ugliness becomes a very horror and scares anything which has the curiosity or rashness to approach and threaten them.

"What are you going to do in Alaska or British Columbia, Tom?" said he to me one day. "Do you think of farming, or seal-hunting, or gold-mining, or what? I should like to hear your plans, if you have any." And then he went on without waiting for an answer, showing plainly that he thought that I had none, and was a fool. "And that young idiot Harmer, why didn't he stick to his ship?"

"Because he will never stick to anything, Mr. Fleming," I answered, "though he is a clever young fellow, and fit for other things than sailoring, if I'm a judge. But as for myself I don't think I am, and yet when I make up my mind to a thing, I usually do it."

"You usually succeed, then?" said he, with a hard smile. "It is well to have belief in one's own strength and abilities. But sometimes others have strength as well, and then"——

"And then," I answered, "it is very often a question of will."

He smiled again and dropped the subject.

On the third day out from San Francisco, when we were running along the coast of Oregon, I found at last an opportunity of speaking to Elsie. I first went to Fanny.

"Fanny, my dear girl, I want to speak to you a few minutes." I sat down beside her.

"I think you know, Fanny, why I am here, don't you?" I asked.

"It is tolerably obvious, Mr. Ticehurst," she answered rather gravely, I thought.

"Yes, I suppose it is; but first I want to be sure whether you were right about what you told me on the morning we left San Francisco."

I was silent, and looked at her. She seemed a trifle distressed.

"Well, Tom, I thought that I was," she answered at length; "and I still think I am—and yet I don't know. You see, Elsie is a strange girl, and never confides in anyone since dear mother died, and she would never confess anything to me. Still, I have eyes in my head, and ears too. But since you have been with us she has been harder and colder than I ever saw her in all my life, and she has said enough to make me think that there is something that I know nothing about which makes her so. You know, I joked her about you yesterday, and she got so angry all of a sudden, like pouring kerosene on a fire, and she said you were a coward. When I asked her why, she turned white and wouldn't answer. Then I said of course you must be a coward if she said so, but I didn't think she had any right to say it or think it when you had saved all our lives by your coolness and courage. And then, you know, I got angry and cried, because I like you very much, just as much as I do my brother on the station at home. And I said she was a cruel beast, and all kinds of horrid things, until I couldn't think of anything but making faces at her, just as I did when I was a child. And we are having a quarrel now, and it is all about you—you ought to be proud." And Fanny looked up half laughing and half crying, for she dearly loved Elsie, as I knew.

"Well, my dear little sister Fanny," I said, "for you shall be my sister one day, there is something that makes her think ill of me, but it is not my fault, as far as I can see. And I can't convince her of that, except by showing her that I am not the man she thinks, unless some accident puts me back into the place I once believed I held in her thoughts. But I want to speak to her, and I must do it to-day. To-morrow we shall be in Victoria, and I should not like to part with her without speaking. If I talk with her now, it will probably take some time, so I want you, if you can, to prevent anyone interrupting us."

Fanny nodded, and wiped away a tear in a quick manner, just as if it were a fly.

"Very well, I will. You know I trust you, if Elsie doesn't." And she went over to Harmer, who was in a fidget, and kept looking at me as if he was wondering what I meant by talking so confidentially to Fanny.

I found Elsie sitting by herself just forward of the funnel. She was reading, and though when I spoke she answered and put the book down in her lap, she kept looking at it in a nervous way, as if she wished I had not interrupted her; and we had been talking some minutes before she seemed to wholly forget that it was there.

I spoke without any thought of what I was going to say.

"Miss Fleming (see, I call you that, though a little while ago it was Elsie), I have determined to speak to you in spite of the way you avoid me."

"I would rather you did not, Mr. Ticehurst," she said.

"It has come to a time when I must do as I think fit, even if I am rude and rough. I have something to say, and mean to say it, Miss Fleming; and if I word it in rough or broken fashion, if I stumble over it or stammer with my tongue, you will know why, just as you know why I am here. Come now, why am I on this steamer?"

She remained mute, with her head bent down, and the gold of her hair loose over her eyes, so that I could not see them. But she trembled a little, and was ripping one of the pages of her book. I took hold of it and put it down. She made no remonstrance, and I began to feel that I had power over her, though how far it went I could not tell.

"Why am I here?" I went on scornfully. "Oh, on a pleasure trip to see the advertised coast from San Francisco to Sitka, to behold Mount Elias and its glaciers! By Heavens, I think I have ice nearer at hand! Oh, it is business? I wish to gain wealth, so I give up what I understand, and go into what is as familiar to me as a sextant is to a savage! It can't be business. Do you know what it is, Miss Fleming? Look, I think there was a girl who I knew once, but she was a kind, bright girl, who was joyous, whom I called by her Christian name, who walked by my side in the moonlight, when the sails were silvered and their shadows dark, when I kept the first watch in the *Vancouver*. I wonder what has become of her? That girl would have known, but——"

I stopped, and she was still stubborn. But she did not move. I went on again:

"There must be evil spirits on the sea that fly like petrels in the storm, and come on board ship and enter into the hearts of those they find there. Why——"

"I fear, Mr. Ticehurst," she interrupted, "that you think me a fool. If I am not, then your talk is vain; and if I am, I surely am not fit to mate with you. Let us cease to talk about this, for it is useless!"

I was almost choking with passion; it was so hard to be misconceived, even though she had so much reason on her side. Yet, since I knew she was wrong, I almost wished to shake her.

"No!" I said at last, "I will not go until I have an understanding one way or the other. We have been beating about the bush, but I will do it no longer. You know that I love you!"

She drew herself up.

"How many can you love at a time, Mr. Ticehurst?" she said.

"One, only one," I replied. "You are utterly mistaken."

"I am not mistaken!" she said; "and I think you are a coward and a traitor. If you were not, I might love you; but as you are, such a thing is impossible."

I caught her by the wrist. Instinctively she tried to free herself, but finding she could not, looked up. When she caught my eye, her indignant remonstrance died on her lips.

"Look you, Elsie, what can I do? Perhaps I cannot defend myself; there are some situations where a man cannot for the sake of others. I can say no more about that. And I will make you see you are wrong, if not by proof, by showing you what I am—a man incapable of what you think me—and in the end I will make you love me." I paused for a moment, but she did not move.

"You have listened to me; Elsie, and you can see what I mean, you can think whether I shall falter or swerve; and now I ask you, for I am assured you do love me, or that you did, whether you will not trust me now? For you cannot believe that I could speak as I do if I had done what you think."

I looked at Elsie, and she was very pale. I could see that I had moved her, had shaken her conviction, that she was at war with herself. I got up, went to the side, and then turned, beckoning to her to look over to seaward with me. She came almost like a woman walking in her sleep, and took a place by my side. I did so to avoid notice, for I feared to attract attention; indeed, I saw two passengers looking at us curiously, one of whom smiled so that I began to wish to throw him overboard. Yet I think, as a matter of fact, I did wrong in allowing her to move; it broke the influence I held over her in a measure, for I have often noticed since that to obtain control of some people one should keep steadily insisting on the one point, and never allow them to go beyond, or even to think beyond it. But then to do so one must be stronger than I was, or he will lose control over himself, as I did, and so make errors in judgment.

"Elsie," I said quietly, "are you not going to answer me? Or am I not worth it?"

Now, up to this moment I had taken her away from the past; in her emotion she had almost forgotten Helen; she was just wavering and was on the point of giving in to me. Yet by that last suggestion of mine I brought it back to her. I could see in her mind the darker depths of her fear and distrust of me, and what I rightly judged her hatred and jealousy of Helen. Though I do not think I know much of character, yet in the state of mind that I was in then I seemed to see her mind, as a much more subtle man might have done, and my own error. I could have cursed my own folly. She had taken the book again, and was holding it open in her hand. Until I spoke she held it so lightly that it shook and wavered, but she caught it in both hands and shut it suddenly, as though it was the book of her heart that I had been reading, and she denied my right to do it. And she turned toward me cold once more, though by a strange influence she caught my thought.

"This is a closed book, Mr. Ticehurst. It is the book of the past, and—it is gone for ever." She dropped it over the side with a mocking smile. But I caught hold of her hand and held it.

"Ah!" said I, "then we begin again. If the past is dead, the present lives, and the future is yet unborn. You mean one thing now, and I mean the other; but in the future we shall both mean the same. Remember what I say, Elsie—remember it. For unless I am dead, I will be your acknowledged lover and your husband at last."

I dropped her hand and walked away, and when I looked back I saw her following me with her eyes. I would have given much then to have been able to know of what she thought. I went below and slept for many hours a sleep of exhaustion, for though a man may be as strong as a lion physically, an excess of emotion takes more from him than the most terrible physical toil.

The next morning we were in Victoria, and I neither had, nor did I seek, an opportunity of again speaking with Elsie. But I did talk for a few moments with Fanny. I told her some part of what occurred, but not much. She said as much:

"You are keeping something back, Tom. I think you know some reason why Elsie won't have anything to do with you?"

"I do, Fanny," I replied: "but there is nothing in it at all, and one of these days she will discover it."

"I hope so," said she, a little dryly for so young a girl; "but Elsie is a little obstinate, and I have seen horses that would not jump a gate. You may have to open it yet, Tom."

"It may open of it itself, Fanny, or the horse may desire the grass and jump at last; but I will never open it myself."

And I shook hands with her and Mr. Fleming. I took off my hat to Elsie, but said in a low voice:

"Remember what I said, Elsie, for I shall never forget." And then she turned away; but did not look back this time, as she had done when we parted in the hotel. Yet such is the curious state a lover is in that I actually comforted myself that she did not, for if she had, I said, it would have showed she was callous and cold. Perhaps, though she kept command over herself just for the time, it failed her at the last, and she would not let me see it.

When they were gone, Harmer and I went ashore too. As to the boy, he was so desperately in love—calf-love—that I had to cheer him up, and the way I did it makes me laugh now, for I have a larger experience of boys and men than I had then.

"Never mind, Harmer," said I, "you will get over this in no time—see if you don't."

He turned round in a blazing rage, and I think if it had not been for the effects of the old discipline, which was yet strong upon him, he would have sworn at me; for although Harmer looked as if butter wouldn't melt in his mouth, I knew he had a very copious vocabulary of abuse at his command, such as one learns only too easily at sea.

"What, Mr. Ticehurst!" he said stammering. "Get over it? I never shall, and I don't want to, and, what's more, I wouldn't if I could! It's not kind of you to say so, and I think—I think——"

"What, Jack?" said I, thunderstruck at this outburst, when I meant consolation.

"That you'll get over it first. There now!" said he, triumphant with this retort I burst into laughter.

"Well—well, Harmer, I didn't mean to vex you. We must not quarrel now, for Jordan's a hard road to travel, I believe, and you and I have got to make lots of money; at least you have; if we are going to do anything in this country. For it's what the Yankees call a tough place."

"Yes," replied Harmer, now ashamed of of being angry. "I heard one fellow say to another on the steamer, 'You goldarned fellers from the East think you're going to get a soft seat over here, but you bet you'll have to rustle on the Pacific Slope or else git!' And then he turned to me. 'D'ye hear that, young feller?—you've got to rustle right smart, or you'll get left.'"

And Jack laughed heartily trying to imitate the accent of his adviser, but he found it hard to disguise his own pure English, learnt in a home far across the seas and the wide stretch of the American Continent.

That night we stayed in Victoria in a rough hotel kept by two brothers, Cornishmen, who invited us both to have drinks on the strength of our all being Englishman, though I should never have suspected that they were such, so well did their accent disguise the truth from me. And in the morning, two days after, we went on board the *Western Slope* bound for New Westminster, on the mainland of British Columbia, whither the Flemings had preceded us.

PART III. A GOLDEN LINK.

What I have just written is but the connecting link between two series of events—the hyphen between two words; and I shall not try to hurry on to the strange drama of a few days to which all that precedes it has been but the inevitable prologue, without which there were no clear understanding of its incidents. I am going, therefore, to dispose of a whole year's events in a few words, though much occurred in that time which might be worth relating, if I were a professional writer, able to make things interesting to all, or if I had the faculty of making word-pictures of places and scenes which stand out clearly before me whenever I reflect, and the full times of the past come up for review.

What Jack Harmer and I did for that year truly would take ten times the space I have allowed myself, and have been allowed, and I shall say but little now if I can only dispose of that twelve months in a way that places my readers in a position to clearly understand what passed in the thirteenth month after I had landed in British Columbia.

Now on our landing we had but £40 between us, and I was the possessor of nearly all that amount, about two hundred dollars in American currency. It is true I had a hundred and fifty pounds in England, which I had sent for, and Harmer had quite coolly asked his father for fifty, which I may state here he did *not* get in a letter which advised him to return to England, and go in for something worth having before it was too late.

"He means the Civil Service, I know," said Jack, when he read the letter; "and I hate the notion. They are all fossils in it, and if they have brains to start with, they rarely keep them—why should they? They're not half as much use as a friend at court."

Perhaps he was right, yet I advised him to take his father's advice, and he took neither his nor mine, but stuck to me persistently with a devotion that pleased and yet annoyed me. For I desired a free hand, and with him I could not get it. I had some idea of going in for farming when I landed. I would get a farm near Elsie's father, and stay there. But I found I hadn't sufficient money, or anything like sufficient, to buy land near Thomson Forks. So I looked round, and, in looking round, spent money. Finally, I got Harmer something to do in a sawmill on Burrard's Inlet, a position which give him sufficient to live on, but very little more; and yet he had not to work very hard, in fact he tallied the lumber into the ships loading in the Inlet for China and Australia, and wrote to me that he liked his job reasonably well, though he was grieved to be away from me. As for myself, I went up to Thomson Forks, looked round me there, and at the hotel fell in with a man named Mackintosh, an American from Michigan, a great strong fellow, with a long red beard, and an eye like an eagle's, who was going up in the Big Bend gold-hunting, prospecting as they call it. I told him, after we got into conversation, that I wanted to go farming.

He snorted scornfully, and immediately began to dilate on gold-mining and all the chances a man had who possessed the grit to tackle it. And as I knew I really had too little money to farm with, it wasn't long before he persuaded me to be his partner and go with him. For I liked him at once, and was feeling so out in the cold that I was glad to chum with anyone who looked like knowing his way about. We were soon in the thick of planning our campaign, and Mac got very fluent and ornamental in his language as he drank and talked. However, I did not mind that much, although his blasphemy was British Columbian, and rather worse than that in use on board ship. Yet people do not think the sea a mean school of cursing. Presently, as I turned round at the bar, I saw Mr. Fleming, who did not notice me until I spoke.

"Good-morning, Mr. Fleming," I said; "will you drink with me?"

He turned round sharply at the sound of my voice, and then shook my hand, half doubtfully at first, and then more heartily.

"Well, Ticehurst," he said at last, "I am glad to see you, after all. Hang it, I am! for" (here he lowered his voice to a whisper) "I don't care about the style of this place after New South Wales. They nearly all carry revolvers here, damn it! as if they were police; and last time I came in, my man and another fellow fought, and Siwash Jim (that's what they call him) tried to gouge out the other chap's eyes. And when I pulled him off, the other men growled about my spoiling a fight. What do you think of that?"

And the old man stared at me inquiringly, and then laughed.

"Wish I could ask you over to the Creek, but I can't, and you know why. Take my advice and go back to sea. Now, look here, let's speak plain. I know you want Elsie; but it's a mistake, my boy. She didn't care for you; and I know her, she's just like her mother, the obstinatest woman you ever saw when she made up her mind. I wouldn't mind much if she did care for you, though perhaps you aint so rich as you ought to be, Tom. But then my wife had more money than I had by a long sight, so I don't care for that. But seeing that Elsie doesn't want you, what's the use? Take my advice and go to sea again."

Here he stopped and gave me the first chance of speaking I had had since

I accosted him.

"Thank you, Mr. Fleming," I said firmly; "but I can't go back yet. I am glad you have no great objection to me yourself, but I believe that Elsie hasn't either, and I'm bound to prove it; and I will."

"Well, you know best," he replied. "But mind your eye, old boy, when your friend the Malay comes out. I shouldn't like to be on the same continent with him, if I were you."

"I don't like being either," I said. "But then it shows how fixed I am on one object. And I shall not go, even if he were to find out where I am. For I might have to kill him. Yet I don't see how he can find out. Nobody knows or will know, except my brother, and he won't tell him."

Fleming shrugged his shoulders and dropped the subject to take up his own affairs.

"Damn this country, my boy! give me a plain where I can see a few miles. On my soul, this place chokes me; I can't look out five hundred yards for some thundering old mountain! At the Creek there are hills at the back, at the front, and on both sides, and nearly all are chokeful of trees, so that riding after the cattle is worse than going after scrub cattle in Australia. I can't get the hang of the place at all, and though I am supposed to own nearly two hundred head of cattle, I can't muster seventy-five on my own place. Some are up at Spullamacheen, some on the Nicola, and others over at the Kettle River on the border, for all I know. And the place is full of cañons, as they call gulches in this place; and thundering holes they are, two hundred feet deep, with a roaring stream at the bottom. The Black Cañon at the back of my place gives me the shivers. I am like a horse bred on the plains; when it gets on the mountains it is all abroad, and shivers at the sight of a sharp slope. I reckon I can ride on the flat, old as I am, but here, if it wasn't for my scoundrel Siwash Jim, who says he knows the country like a book, I shouldn't know where to go or what to do. Here he comes, the vagabond!"

I had learnt by this time that Siwash means Indian, for in that country they say Siwashes instead of Indians, so I thought Jim was one of the natives. However, I saw at once he wasn't, for though he was dark, his features were pure white. He had earned his nickname by living with the Indians for so many years that he was more at home with them than with white people, and he had acquired all their vices as well as a goodly stock of his own, probably inherited. He was a slightly built man of about forty, with a low forehead, a sharp aquiline nose, and no lips to speak of; his mustache was short, and a mere line; his teeth were black with smoking and chewing; his legs bowed with continual riding. He wore mocassins, and kept his hair long. He was more than half intoxicated when he came in, carrying a stock-whip coiled round his neck. He did not speak, but drank stolidly; and when he looked at me, I fancied it was with an air of dislike, as though he had read my thoughts and knew how I regarded him.

I drew Fleming aside.

"I don't like him," said I; "and wouldn't trust him farther than I could swing a bull by the tail. Do the girls like him?"

"Like him!" repeated Fleming, "they hate him, and want me to give him the bounce, as they say here. Elsie says he looks like a murderer, and Fanny that he is uglier than a Murrumbidgee black fellow. But then he knows the country and does his work, and don't want to go. I don't care much either way, for when I can get all the cattle together and put the place in order I shall sell out and go back. Stay in British Columbia—no, sir, I won't! not if they make me Governor. I tell you I like to be where I can see ten miles. Then I can breathe. I can go out at home and see all my station and almost count the sheep and cattle from my door; and here I have to ride up and ride down, and I never know where I am. I'm going back just as soon as I can."

And he went away then without asking where I was going or whether I was doing anything. Next morning I jumped on board the steamer with Mac and started for the head of the Shushwap Lakes. Thence we went into the Big Bend, and though we never made the millions Mac was always prophesying about and hungering for, our summer's work was not wasted. For before the season was over we had struck a rich pocket and made about four thousand dollars a piece.

Of course I wanted to up stick and go back as soon as I had as much as that, but Mac would not hear of it.

"No, Tom—no," said he; "there's more here yet."

And he eyed me so entreatingly that I caved in and promised to remain with him prospecting, at any rate till the first snow.

But a week after making that agreement we both went down to the Columbia for more provisions. Finding none there, we had to make the farther journey to the Landing. There I found a letter waiting for me from Harmer, saying that he was tired of the sawmill on the Inlet, and wanted to join me. I wrote back requesting him to be good enough to stay where he was, but, to console him, promised that if I saw any chance of his doing better with me I would send for him. He asked rather timidly for news of Fanny. How could I give him news when I knew nothing of Elsie? Yet the simple mention of the girl's name again made me anxious to get back to the Forks, and if one of the steamers had come up the lake I think I should have deserted Mac in spite of my promise. Yet we had only brought down half the gold that trip, perhaps because my partner had made a calculation as to what I might do, having it on me, if we got within reach of some kind of civilization, and I thought it best to secure the rest while I could, though I thoroughly trusted Mac. At the same time that I answered Harmer's letter I wrote one to my brother, telling him both what I had done and what I proposed doing later on. And I begged him to be careful, if he should be in San Francisco then, of the Malay when his time was up. For although his chief spite was against me, yet Will was my brother, and I well remembered the look that he had cast on him when he was kicked in the struggle between Will and myself.

The rest of the summer—and a beautiful season it was in the wooded mountains—was spent in very unsuccessful prospecting. For one thing, after our success Mac had taken to prospecting for pockets; and if gold-mining be like gambling as a general rule, that is almost pure chance. Once or twice he was in high spirits at good indications, but on following them up we were invariably disappointed, and we had to start again. August and September passed, and the higher summits above us were already white with snow, which fell on us in the lower valleys as rain. In October there was a cessation of bad weather for a time, and Mac promised himself a long fall season, but at the end of it we woke one morning to find a foot of snow on our very camping ground.

"We shall have to get up and get," said I cheerfully, for I was glad of it.

"Oh, no!" said Mac; "this is nothing. It will all go again by to-morrow; there will be nothing to stop us from another week or two. Besides, yesterday I had a notion that I saw something. I didn't tell you, but I found another bit of quartz—aye, richer than the piece I showed you at the Forks, Tom, and we've got to find out where it comes from."

I groaned, but, in spite of argument, there was no moving him; and though I was angry enough to have gone off by myself, yet knowing neither the trail nor the country well, I had no desire to get lost in the mountains, which would most assuredly have meant death to me. However, I still remonstrated, and at last got him to fix ten days as the very longest time he would remain: I was obliged to be content with that.

But Mac was sorry before the hour appointed for our departure that he had not taken my advice, "tenderfoot" and Englishman though I was. On the evening of the eighth day the temperature, which had up to that time been fairly warm in spite of our altitude and the advanced season, fell suddenly, and it became bitterly cold. Our ponies, who had managed to pick up a fair living on the plateau where our camp stood, and along the creek bottoms, came right up to our tent, and one of them put his head inside. "Dick," as we called him, was a much gentler animal than most British Columbian cayuses, and had made a friend of me, coming once a day at least for me to give him a piece of bread, of which he had grown fond, though at first he was as strange with it as a young foal with oats. I put up my hand and touched his nose, which was soft and silky, while the rest of his coat was long and rough. He whinnied gently, and I found a crust for him, and then gently repulsing him, I fastened the fly of the tent. Mac was fast asleep under his dark blankets, whence there came sudden snorts like those a bear makes in his covert, or low rumblings like thunder from a thick cloud.

But it was he who woke me in the morning, and he did it without ceremony.

"Get up, old man!" he said hurriedly, while he was jamming himself, as it were, into his garments. "The snow's come at last—and, by thunder, it's come to stay! There's no time to be lost!" And he vanished into the white space outside.

When I followed I found him already at work packing the ponies, and without any words I set to, struck the tent, rolled it up, and got together everything I thought should go. When I touched the tools Mac turned round.

"Leave 'em, pard—leave 'em. There's plenty of weight without that. Aye, plenty—and too much!"

The last I only just caught, for it was said to himself. In half an hour we were off, leaving behind us nearly three weeks' provisions, all the tools but two light shovels, and what remained after our working the quartz.

"It's worth a thousand dollars," said Mac, regretfully, "but without a proper crusher it's only tailings."

We moved off camp, Mac first, leading the nameless pony, which was the stronger of the two, and I following with Dick.

The snow was two feet deep in many parts, and in some drifts much more than that. Fortunately, the trail was for its greater length well sheltered, both by overhanging rocks and big trees, spruce, cedar, hemlock, and pine, which helped to keep it clear; but it was evident to me by the way the ponies traveled, and the labor it was for me to get along with no other burden than the shovel, from which I sometimes used to free Dick, that another fall of snow would make traveling almost impossible. Mac walked on in somber silence, reflecting doubtless that it was his obstinacy which had brought us into trouble, a thing I confess I was not so forgiving as to forget, though merciful enough not to remind him of it. It had taken us three days to come up from the Columbia, and it seemed barely possible under the circumstances to retrace our steps in the same time, even although the horses were not so much burdened and there was not so much hard climbing to be done. But I could see Mac was bent on getting out, and he traveled without more rest than we were absolutely compelled to take on account of the animals. As for myself, I confess that though I had traveled that same trail twice, yet so greatly was it altered by the snow that I should have lost my way in the first mile. For mountaineering and the knowledge of locality are things not to be learnt in a hurry, they must come by long custom, or by native instinct.

Sorrowfully—for I am always loth to harm even a noxious animal, as long as it leaves me alone—I suggested to Mac that we should leave the horses. He shook his head.

"Who'll carry the provisions, then?" said he.

"Do you think we can get to the Landing, Mac?" I asked.

"We shall be lucky," he answered, with a significant nod, "if we get to the other side of the Columbia. Tom, I think I have let you in for a winter up here, unless you care about snow-shoeing it over the other pass. I was a fool—say yes to that if you like."

It was late when we camped, but my partner was in better spirits than he had been at noon when we held the above conversation, for we had done, by dint of forced marching, quite as much as we did in fine weather. But the ponies were very tired, and there was nothing for them to eat, or next to nothing, for the grass was deeply buried. I gave Dick a little bread, however, and the poor animal was grateful for it, and stood by me all night, until, at the earliest dawn, we packed them again with a load that was lighter by the day's food of two men, and heavier to them by a day's hard toil and starvation.

Toward the afternoon of that, the second day, we came to the hardest part of the whole trail, for, on crossing a river which was freezing cold, we had to climb the side of an opposing mountain. Mac's pony traveled well, and though he showed evident signs of fatigue, he was in much better case than mine, who every now and again staggered, or sobbed audibly with a long-drawn breath. I drew Mac's attention to it, but he shook his head.

"He must go on, there's no two ways about it." And he marched off. I went behind Dick and pushed him for a while, and though I tired myself, yet I am not sorry for what I did, even that little assistance was such a relief to the poor wretched animal who, from the time he was able to bear a weight, had been used by a packer without rest or peace, as though he were a machine, and whose only hope of release was to die, starved, wounded, saddle and girth galled, of slow starvation at last. Such is the lot of the pack horse, and, though poor Dick's end was more merciful, his fellows have no better fate to expect, while their life is a perpetual round of ill-usage and hard work.

By about four o'clock in the afternoon the sky grew overcast, and the light feathery flakes of snow came at first slowly, and then faster, turning what blue distances we caught sight of to a gray, finally hiding them. Dick by this time was almost at a standstill. I never thought I was a very tender-hearted man, and never set up to be; indeed, if he had been only stubborn, I might have thrashed him in a way some folks would call cruel; and yet, being compelled to urge him, both for his sake and my own, I confess my heart bled to see his suffering and wretchedness. Having scarcely the strength to lift his feet properly, he had struck his fetlocks against many projecting stones and roots until the blood ran down and congealed on his little hoofs, which were growing tender, as I could see by the way he winced on a rockier piece of the trail than common. His rough coat was standing up and staring like that of a broken-haired terrier, in spite of the sweat which ran down his thin sides and heaving flanks; while every now and again he stumbled, and with difficulty recovered himself.

When we came to the divide, just as if he had said that he would do so much for us, he stumbled again, and fell on the level ground, cutting his knees deeply. Mac heard the noise, and, leaving his pony standing, he came back to me.

"He's done up, poor devil!" said he; "he'll go no further. What shall we do?"

I shook my head, for it was not I who arranged or ordered things when Mac was about. He was silent for a while.

"There's nothing for it," he said at last, "but one thing. We must put all the other kieutan can stand on him."

By this time I had got the pack off Dick, and he lay down perfectly flat upon his side, with the blood slowly oozing from his knees, and his flanks still heaving from the exertions which had brought him up the hill to die on the top of it.

"Come on," said Mac, as he moved off with what he meant to put on the other pony.

But at first I could not go. I put my hand in my pocket, took out a piece of bread, and, kneeling down by the poor animal, I put it to his lips. He mumbled it with his teeth and dropped it out. Then in my hat I got some water out of a little pool and offered it to him. He drank some and then fell back again. I took my revolver from my belt, stroked his soft nose once more, and, putting the weapon to his head between his eye and ear, I fired. He shivered all over, stiffened a little, and all was still except for the slow drip of the blood that ran out of his ear from a vein the ball had divided. Then I went on—and I hope no one will think me weak if I confess my sight was not quite so clear as it had been before, and if there was a strange haziness about the cruelly cold trail and mountain side that did not come from the falling snow.

At our camp that night we spoke little more than was absolutely necessary, and turned in as soon as we had eaten supper, drunk a tin of coffee, and smoked a couple of pipes. Fortunately for the remaining horse, in the place we had reached there was a little feed, a few tussocks of withering frost-nipped bunch grass, which he ate greedily to the last roots his sharp teeth could reach. And then he pawed or "rustled" for more, using his hoof to bare what was hidden under the snow. But for that we should have left him on the trail next morning.

The toil and suffering of the third day's march were dreadful, for I grew footsore, and my feet bled at the heels, while the skin rose in blisters on every toe, which rapidly became raw. But Mac was a man of iron, and never faltered or grew tired; and his example, and a feeling of shame at being outdone by another, kept me doggedly behind him at a few paces' distance. How the pony stood that day was a miracle, for he must have been made of iron and not flesh and blood to carry his pack, while climbing up and sliding down the steep ascents and slopes of the hills, while every few yards some wind-felled tree had to be clambered over almost as a dog would do it. He was always clammy with sweat, but he seemed in better condition than on the second day, perhaps on account of the grass he had been able to get during the night. Yet he had had to work all night to get it, while I and Mac had slept in the torpor of great exhaustion.

Late in the evening we came to the banks of the Columbia, across which stretched sandy flats and belts of scrub, until the level ended, and lofty mountains rose once more, covered with snow and fringed with sullen clouds, thousands of feet above where we stood. Mac stopped, and looked anxiously across the broad stream; and when he saw a faint curl of bluish smoke rising a mile away in the sunless air, he pointed to it with a more pleased expression that I had seen on his face since he had roused me so hurriedly on that snowy morning three days ago.

"There is somebody over there, at any rate, old man," he said almost cheerfully, "though I don't know what the thunder they're doing here, unless it's Montana Bill come up trapping. He said he was going to do it, but if so, what's he doing down here?"

"Can't he trap here, then?" I asked.

"Well," replied Mac, "this might be the end of his line; but still, he ought to be farther up in the hills. There isn't much to trap close down on this flat. You see trappers usually have two camps, and they walk the line during the day, and take out what is caught in the night, setting the traps again, and sleeping first at one end and then at the other. However, we shall see when we get across." And he set about lighting a fire.

When we had crossed before there had been a rough kind of boat built out of pine slabs, which was as crazy a craft to go in as a butter-tub. It had been made by some hunters the winter before, and left there when they went west in the early spring, before we came up. I asked Mac what had become of it, for it was not where we had left it, hauled up a little way on a piece of shingle and tied to a stump.

"Somebody took it," he said, "or more likely, when the water rose after we crossed, it was carried away. Perhaps it's in the Pacific by this."

I went down to the stump, and found there the remains of the painter, and as it had been broken violently and not cut, I saw that his last suggestion was probably correct.

We sat down to supper by our fire, which gleamed brightly in the gathering darkness on the surrounding snow and the waters close beneath us, and ate some very vile bacon and a greasy mess of beans which we had cooked the night before we left our mountain camp.

"How are we going to cross, Mac?" said I, when we had lighted our pipes.

"Build a raft," said he.

"And then?"

"When we are over?"

"Yes."

"Why, stay there, I guess, if it snows any more. One more fall of heavy snow will block Eagle Pass as sure as fire's hot!"

I shrugged my shoulders. Though I had been expecting this, it was not pleasant to have the prospect of spending a whole winter mewed up in the mountains, so close before me.

"Does it get very cold here?" I asked at length, when I had reflected for a while.

He nodded sardonically.

"Does it get cold? Is it cold now?"

I drew closer to the fire for an answer.

"Then this is nothin'—nothin' at all. It would freeze the tail off a brass monkey up here. It goes more than forty below zero often and often; and it's a worse kind of cold than the cold back east, for it's damper here, and not so steady. Bah! I wish I was a bear, so as to hole up till spring."

All of which was very encouraging to a man who had mostly sailed in warm latitudes, and hated a frost worse than poison. And it didn't please me to see that so good-tempered a man as Mac was really put out and in a vile humor, for he knew what I could only imagine.

The conversation—if conversation it could be called—flagged very soon, and we got out our blankets, scraping away the snow from a place, where we lay close to each other in order to preserve what warmth we could. We lay in the position commonly called in America "spooning," like two spoons fitting one into another, so that there had to be common consent for changing sides, one of which grew damp while the other grew cold. Just as we were settling down to sleep we heard the sudden crack of a rifle from the other shore, and against the wind came a "halloa" across the water, Mac sat up very unconcernedly; but, as for me, I jumped as if I had been shot, thinking of course at first that the shot had been fired by Indians, though I knew there were no hostile tribes in that part of British Columbia, where, indeed, most of the Indians are very peaceable.

"I told you so," said Mac; "that's Montana Bill's rifle. I sold it him myself. He's the only man up here that carries a Sharp."

He rose, and went down to the water's edge. "Halloa!" he shouted, in his turn, and in the quietness of the windless air I heard it faintly repeated in distant echoes.

"Is that you, Mac?" said the mysterious voice.

"You bet it is!" answered my partner, in a tone that ought to have been heard on the Arrow Lake.

"Bully old boy!" said Bill faintly, as it seemed. "Do you know me?"

"Aye, I reckon I know old Montana's bellow!" roared Mac.

"Then I'll see you in the morning, pard!" came the voice again, after which there was silence, broken only by the faint lap of the water on the shingle, as it slipped past, and the snort of our pony as he blew the snow out of his nostrils, vainly seeking for a tuft of grass.

We rose at earliest dawn, and saw Montana Bill slowly coming over the level. He sat down while Mac and I built a raft, and fashioned a couple of rude paddles with the ax.

"Is the pony coming across, Mac?" I asked.

"We'll try it, but it's his own lookout," said he; "if he won't come easy we shan't drag him, for we shall hev to paddle to do it ourselves."

Fortunately for him he did want to go over, and, having a long lariat round his neck, he actually swam in front of us, and gave us a tow instead of our giving him one.

As we were going over, Mac said to me:

"I never thought I'd be glad to see Montana Bill before. He's got more gas and blow about him than'd set up a town, and he's no more good at bottom—that is, he aint no more grit in him than a clay bank, though to hear him talk you'd think he'd mor'n a forty-two inch grindstone. But I hope he's got a good stock of grub."

In a few minutes we touched bottom, and we shook hands with the subject of Mac's eulogium, who looked as bold as brass, as fierce as a turkeycock, and had the voice of a man-o'-war's bo'son. We took the lariat off the pony, and turned him adrift.

"Did you fellows strike it?" said Bill, the first thing.

"Enough to pay for our winter's board, I reckon," said Mac. "Have you got plenty of grub?"

Bill nodded, using the common American word for yes, which is a kind of cross-breed between "yea" and the German "Ja," pronounced short like "ye."

"You bet I've plenty. Old Hank kem up with me, and then he cleared out again. He and I kind of disagreed first thing, and he just skinned out. Good thing too—for him!"

And Bill looked unutterable things.

"Is there any chance of getting out over the pass?" asked Mac.

"If you can fly," answered Bill. "Drifts is forty foot deep in parts, and soft too. I could hardly get on snow-shoein' it. Better stay and trap with me. Better'n gold-huntin' any time, and more dollars in it."

"Why aint you farther up in the hills?" asked Mac, as we tramped along.

"Dunno," said Bill; "I allers camp here every year. It's kind of clear, and there's a chance for the cayuses to pick a bit to keep bones and hide together. Besides, I feel more freer down here. I see more than 'ull do me of the hills walking the line."

And with that we came to his camp.

Now, if I tell all that happened during that winter, which was, all round, the most uncomfortable and most unhappy one I ever spent, for I had so much time to think of Elsie, and how some other man more to her mind might go to windward of me in courting her—why, I should not write one book, but two, which is not my intention now. Besides, I have been long enough coming to the most serious part of my history to tire other people, as it has tired me; although I could not exactly help it, because all, or at least nearly all, that happened between the time I was on the *Vancouver* and the time we all met again seems important to me, especially as it might have gone very differently if I had never been gold-hunting in the Selkirks, or even if I had got out of the mountains in the fall instead of the following spring. For things seem linked together in life, and, in writing, one must put everything in unless more particular description becomes tedious, because of its interfering with the story. And though trapping is interesting enough, yet I am not writing here about that or hunting, which is more interesting still; and when a man tells me a yarn he says is about a certain thing, I don't want him to break off in the middle to say something quite different, any more than I like a man to get up in the middle of a job of work, such as a long splice which is wanted, to do something he wasn't ordered to do. It's only a way of doing a literary Tom Cox's traverse, "three times round the deck house, and once to the scuttle-butt"—just putting in time, or making what a literary friend of mine calls "padding."

So folks who read this can understand why I shall say nothing of this long and weary winter, and, if they prefer it, they can think that we "holed up," as Mac said, like the bears, and slept through it all. For in the next part of this yarn it will be spring, with the snow melting fast, and the trail beginning to look like a path again that even a sailor, who was not a mountaineer, could hope to travel on without losing his life, or even his way.

PART IV. LOVE AND HATE.

It had been raining for a week in an incessant torrent, while the heavy clouds hung low down the slopes of the sullen, sunless mountains, when we struck camp in the spring-time, and loaded our gaunt pack-ponies for the rapidly opening trail. Our road lay for some twenty miles on the bottom of a flat, which closed in more and more as we went east, until we were in the heart of the Gold Range. The path was liquid mud, in which we sank to the tops of our long boots, sometimes even leaving them embedded there; and the ponies were nearly "sloughed down" a dozen times in the day. At the worst places we were sometimes compelled to take off their packs, which we carried piecemeal to firmer ground, and there loaded them again. It had taken us but four or four and a half days to cross it on our last trip, and now we barely reached Summit Lake in the same time.

Yet, in spite of the miserable weather and our dank and dripping condition, in spite of the hard work and harder idleness, when wind and rain made it almost impossible to sleep, I was happy—far happier than I had been since the time I had so miserably failed to make Elsie believe what I told her; for now I was going back to her with the results of my long toil, and there was nothing to prevent my staying near her, perhaps on a farm of my own, until she should recognize her error at last. Yet, I thought it well to waste no time, for though I had to a great extent got rid of my fears concerning that wretched Matthias, still his imprisonment had but a few more months to run, and he *might* keep his word and his sworn oath. I wished to win her and wear her before that time, and after that, why, I did not care, I would do my best, and trust in Providence, even if I trusted in vain.

I have often thought since that it was strange how much John Harmer was in my mind, from daylight even to dark, during the sixth day of our toilsome tramp over Eagle Pass, for his image often unaccountably came before me, and even dispossessed the fair face of her whom I loved. But it was so, and no time during that day should I have been very much surprised, though perhaps a little angry, to see him come round a bend in the trail, saying half humbly and half impudently, as he approached me, "How do you do, Mr. Ticehurst?" I almost began to believe after that day in second sight, clairvoyance, and all the other mysterious things which most sensible people look upon as they do on charlatanry and the juggling in a fair, for my presentiments came true in such a strange way; even if it was only an accident or mere coincidence after all. Yet I have seen many things put down as "coincidences" which puzzled me, and wiser people than Tom Ticehurst.

We had camped in a wretchedly miserable spot, which had nothing to recommend it beyond the fact that there really was some grass there; for the wall of rock on our right, which both Mac and Bill considered a protection from the wind, acted as break-winds often do, and gave us two gales in opposite directions, instead of one. So the wind, instead of sweeping over us and going on its way, fought and contended over our heads, and only ceased for a moment to rush skrieking again about our ears as it leapt on the fire and sent the embers here and there, while the rain descended at every possible angle. Perhaps it was on account of the fizzing of the water in the fire, the rattle of the branches overhead, and the whistling of the wind, that we heard no one approaching our grumbling company until they were right upon us. I was just then half a dozen paces out in the darkness, cutting up some wood for our fire, and as the strangers approached the light, I let fall my ax so that it narrowly escaped cutting off my big toe, for one of the two I saw was a boy, and that boy John Harmer! I slouched my big hat down over my eyes, and with some wood in my arms I approached the group and replenished the fire. John was talking with quite a Western twang, as though he was determined not to be taken for an Englishman.

"Rain!" he was saying; "well, you bet it's something like it! On the lake it takes an old hand to know which is land and which is water. Old Hank was nearly drowned in his tent the other day."

"Serve him right!" growled Bill. "But who are you, young feller?—I never see you before, and I mostly know everybody in this country."

Harmer looked up coolly, and taking off his hat, swung it round.

"Well," he answered, "I aint what you'd call celebrated in B.C. yet, and so you mightn't have heard of me. But if you know everybody, perhaps you know Tom Ticehurst and can tell me where he is to be found. For I am looking for him."

"Oh, you are, are you?" said Bill. "Then what's he been doing that you want him so bad as to come across in this trail this weather?"

"He hasn't been doing anything that I know, pard," said Jack; "but I know he was up here with a man named Mackintosh."

"Ah! I know him," replied Bill, "in fact, I've seen him lately. Is Tom Ticehurst a little chap with red hair and a squint?"

"No, he isn't!" shouted Jack, as if he had been libeled instead of me. "He's a good looking fellow, big enough to eat you."

"Oh, is he?" sneered the joker. "I tell you what, young feller, it would take a big man to chew up Montana Bill's little finger."

Harmer burst out laughing.

"So you're Montana Bill, are you?" said he.

"I am," answered Bill as gravely as if it were a kingly title.

"Well, then, old Hank said he could eat you up without pepper or salt. He's as mad at you as a man can be; says he's been practicing shooting all the winter on purpose to do you up, and he puts a new edge on his knife every morning."

"That'll do, young feller," put in Mac, seeing that Bill was getting in a rage, and knowing that he was just the man to have a row with a youngster. "You're a little too fast, you are. My name's Mackintosh, if you want anyone of that name."

"Do I want you!" cried Harmer anxiously; "of course I do! Do you know where Ticehurst is?"

"Yes," replied Mac; while I stood close beside Harmer looking down at the fire so that he couldn't see my face—I was laughing so.

"Then where is he? Hang it! has anything happened to him that you fellows make such a mystery about it?" he asked getting a little alarmed, as I could tell by the tone of his voice.

"Well," replied Mac quietly, "I'll tell you. He was up in the hills with me, and we struck it rich—got a lot of gold, we did, you bet we did," he went on in an irritating drawl; "and then came down when the snow flew. We had such a time getting out, young feller, and then at last we came to the Columbia and there——"

"He was drowned?" said Harmer growing pale.

"No, he warn't," replied Mac. "We got across all right, and stayed all winter trapping with Bill here. And let me tell you, young man, you mustn't trifle with Bill. He's a snorter, he is."

I could see "Damn Bill!" almost on Jack's lips, but he restrained it.

"And when the Chinook came up, and the snow began to melt a few days back, we all got ready to cross the range—him, and Bill, and me. That's six days ago. And a better fellow than him you never struck, no, nor will. What do you think, pard?" he asked with a grin, turning to me.

I grunted.

"And, young feller," Mac went on again, "if he's a pardner of yours, or a shipmate—for I can see you're an Englishman—why, I'm glad he's here and safe."

Then suddenly altering his tone, he turned fiercely on Harmer, who jumped back in alarm.

"Why the thunder don't you shake hands with him? There he is a-waitin'."

And John sprang across the fire and caught me by both hands.

"Confound it, Mr. Ticehurst, how very unkind of you!" he said, with tears in his eyes. "I began to think you were dead." And he looked unutterably relieved and happy, but bursting with some news, I could see.

"Wait till supper, Jack," said I; "and then tell me. But I'm glad to see you."

I was too, in spite of his leaving the Inlet without asking me.

As to the man with whom he came, Montana Bill knew him, and they spent their time in bullying the absent Hank Patterson. It appeared that Harmer had hired him to come and hunt for me as far as the Columbia River, in order to bury me decently, as he had been firmly convinced that I was dead, when he learnt no news of me at the Landing.

The whole five of us sat down to beans and bacon; but I and Harmer ate very little because he wanted to tell me something which I was strangely loth to hear, so sure was I that it could be nothing good. It certainly must be bad news to bring even an impulsive youngster from the coast to the Columbia in such weather.

"Well, what is it, Harmer?" said I at last.

He hesitated a moment.

"Is it anything about her?" I asked quietly, lest the others should overhear.

"Who? Miss F.?" he asked. I nodded, and he shook his head.

"It's no such luck," he went on; "but I am so doubtful of what I have to tell you, although a few hours ago I was sure enough that I didn't know how to begin. When Mat's sentence be up, Mr. Ticehurst?"

I had no need to reckon.

"The 15th of August, Jack."

He looked at me, and then bent over toward me.

"It's up already, sir."

"What, is he dead, then?"

"No, sir, but he has escaped."

And he filled his pipe while I gathered myself together. It was dreadfully unfortunate if it were true.

"How do you know this?" I said at length,

"I saw him in New Westminster one night."

"The deuce you did! Harmer, are you sure?"

The lad looked uncomfortable, and wriggled about on his seat, which was the old stump of a tree felled by some former occupants of our camping ground.

"I should have been perfectly sure, if I hadn't thought he was in the penitentiary," he said finally; "but still, I don't think I can have mistaken his face, even though I only caught sight of it just for a moment down in the Indian town. I was sitting in a cabin with two other fellows and some klootchmen, and I saw him pass. There was not much light, and he was going quick, but I jumped up and rushed out after him. But in the rain and darkness he got away, if he thought anyone was following him; or I missed him."

"I'm glad you did, my boy; he would have thought little of putting his knife into you," and here I rubbed my own shoulder mechanically. "Besides, if he had seen you, that would have helped him to track me. But then, how in the name of thunder (as Mac says) did he come here at all! It can't be chance. Did you look up the San Francisco papers to see if anything was reported as to his escape?"

Harmer brightened as if glad to answer that he had done what I considered he ought to have done.

"Yes, sir, I did; but I found nothing about it, nothing at all."

I reflected a little, and saw nothing clearly, after all, but the imperative necessity of my getting down to the Forks. If Mat were loose, why, I should have to be very careful, it was true; but perhaps he might be retaken, though I did not know if a man could be extradited for simply breaking prison. And if he came up country, and couldn't find me, he might take it into his Oriental skull to harm anyone I knew. The thought made me shiver.

"Did you stay at Thomson Forks, Harmer?" I asked, to try and turn the dark current of my thoughts.

He blushed a little.

"Yes, sir, but only a day. I saw no one, though."

"What, not even Fanny?"

"No, but I wrote to her and told her I was going up the Lakes to see what had become of you."

"That was kind of you, Jack," said I; "I mean it was kind of you to come up here. How do you like the country, eh?"

He turned round comically, shrugged his shoulders, and said nothing. I could see that early spring in the mountains did not please him, especially as we were in the Wet Belt.

But if he did not like the country, I found he could stand it well, for he was as hardy as a pack pony, and never complained, not though we were delayed a whole day by the rain, and on our return to the Landing had to go to Thomson Forks in Indian dugouts. When we did arrive there it was fine at last, and the sun was shining brilliantly.

Mac, Harmer, and I were greeted in the friendliest manner at the hotel by Dave, the bar-tender, who was resplendent with a white shirt of the very finest get up, and diamond studs. He stood us drinks at once.

"You're welcome to it, gentlemen, and more too. For we did think down here that you had been lost in the snow. We never expected to hear of you again. I think a young lady round here must have an interest in you, Mr. Ticehurst," said he knowingly, "for only two days ago she called me out and asked more than particularly about you. When I told her nobody knew enough to make a line in 'Local Items,' unless they said, 'Nothing has yet been heard,' I reckon she was sorry."

"Who was it, Dave?" I asked carelessly "Was it Miss Fanny Fleming?"

"No, sir, it was not; it was Miss Fleming herself, and I must say she's a daisy. The best looking girl between the Rocky Mountains and the Pacific, gentlemen! Miss Fanny is nice—a pretty girl I will say; but——" He stopped and winked, so that I could hardly keep from throwing my glass at his carefully combed and oiled head. But I was happy to think that Elsie had asked after me.

In the morning we got horses from Ned Conlan, and rode over to Mr. Fleming's ranch, which was situated in a long low valley, that terminated a mile above his house in a narrow gulch, down which the creek came. On either side were high hills, covered on their lower slopes with bunch grass and bull pines, and higher up with thick scrub, that ran at last into bare rock, on the topmost peaks of which snow lay for nine months of the year. As we approached the farm, we saw a few of the cattle on the opposing slopes; and on the near side of the valley were the farm-buildings and the house itself, which was partly hidden in trees. We tied our horses to the fence, and marched in, as we fancied, as bold as brass in appearance; but if Harmer felt half as uncomfortable as I did, which I doubt, I am sorry for him. The first person we saw was Fanny, and the first thing she did was to upset her chair on the veranda on the top of a sleeping dog, who at first howled, and then made a rush at us barking loudly.

"Down, Di!" cried Fanny. "How dare you! O Mr. Ticehurst, how glad I am you're not dead! And you, too, Mr. Harmer, though no one said you were! Oh, where's father, I wonder—he'll be glad, too!"

"And Elsie, will she be glad as well, Fanny?" I asked. She looked at me slyly, and nodded.

"You'd better ask her, I think. Here comes father."

He rode up on horseback, followed by Siwash Jim, swinging the noose of a lariat in his right hand, as though he had been after horses or cattle.

"Oh, it's you, Tom, is it?" said Fleming, who was looking very well. "I'm glad you're not quite so dead as I was told. And you, Harmer, how are you? Jim, take these gentlemen's horses to the stable. You've come to stay for dinner, of course. I shan't let you go. I heard you did very well gold-gambling last fall. Come in!" For that news went down the country when we went to the Landing for grub.

I followed, wondering a little whether he would have been quite so effusive if I had done badly. But I soon forgot that when I saw Elsie, who had just come out of her room. I thought, when I saw her, that she was a little paler than when we had last met, though perhaps that was due to the unaccustomed cold and the sunless winter; but she more than ever merited the rough tribute which Dave had paid her in Conlan's bar. She was very beautiful to them; but how much more to me, as she came up, a little shyly, and shook hands softly, saying that she was glad that the bad news they had heard of me was not true. I fancied that she had thought of me often during that winter, and perhaps had seen she had been unjust. At any rate, there was a great difference between what she was then and what she was now.

We talked during dinner about the winter, which the three Australians almost cursed; in fact, the father did curse it very admirably, while Elsie hardly reproved his strong language, so much did she feel that forty degrees below zero merited all the opprobrium that could be cast on it. I described our gold-mining adventures and the winter's trapping, which, by the way, had added five hundred dollars to my other money.

I told Fleming that I was now worth, with some I still had at home, more than five thousand dollars, and I could see it gave him satisfaction.

"What do you think of the country now, Mr. Fleming?" I asked; "and how long shall you stay here?"

He shook his head.

"I don't know, my boy," he answered; "I think, in spite of the cold, we shall have to stand another winter here. This summer I must rebuild the barns and stables; there are still a lot of cattle adrift somewhere; and I won't sell out under a certain sum. That's business, you know; and I have just a little about me, though I am an old fool at times, when the girls want their own way."

"What would you advise me to do?" said I, hoping he would give me some advice which I could flatter him by taking. "You see, when one has so much money, it is only the correct thing to make more of it. The question is how to do it."

"That's quite right, Ticehurst—quite right!" said he energetically. "I'm glad you talk like that; your head's screwed on right; you will be well in yet" (an Australian phrase for our "well off"), "I'll bet on that. Well, you can open a store, or go lumbering, or gold-mining, or hunting, or raise cattle, like me."

I pretended to reflect, though I nearly laughed at catching Harmer's eye, for he knew quite well what I wanted to do.

"Yes, Mr. Fleming, you're right. That's nearly all one can do. But as to keeping a store, you see, I've been so accustomed to an open-air life, I don't think it would suit me. Besides, a big man like me ought to do something else than sell trousers! As to gold-mining, I've done that, and been lucky once, which, in such a gambling game, is against me. And hunting or trapping—well, there's nothing great in that. I think I should prefer cattle-raising, if I could do it. I was brought up on a farm in England, and why shouldn't I die on one in British Columbia, or" (and I looked at Elsie) "in Australia?"

"Quite right, Tom," said Fanny, laughing, for she was too cute to miss seeing what I meant.

Mr. Fleming looked at me approvingly.

"You'll die worth a lot yet, Tom Ticehurst. I like your spirit. I was just the same once. Now, I'll tell you what. Did you ever see George Nettlebury at the Forks?"

"No," I replied, "not that I know of."

"I dare say you have," said he; "he's mostly drunk; and Indian Alice, who is always with him, usually has a black eye, as a gentle reminder that she belongs to an inferior race, if she is his wife. Now, he lives about two miles from here, over yonder" (he pointed over the valley). "He has a house—a very dirty one now, it is true; a stable, and a piece of meadow, fenced in, where he could raise good hay if he would mend the fence and keep other folks' cattle out. He told me the other day that he was sick to death of this place, and he wants just enough to go East with, and return to his old trade of shipbuilding. He says he will take $300 for the whole place, with what is on it. That don't amount to much—two cows, one old steer, and a cayuse he rides round on. If you like, we'll go over and see him. You can buy it, and buy some more cattle, and if you have more next winter than you can feed, I'll let you have the hay cheap. What do you say?"

My heart leapt up, but I pretended I wanted time to think about it.

"Then let's ride over now, and you can look at the place," said he; rising.

Harmer would not come, so I left him with the sisters. When we returned I was the owner of the house, stable, two cows, etc., and George Nettlebury was fighting with Indian Alice, to whom he had announced his intention of going East at once, and without her.

"I'm tired of this life; it's quite disgusting!" said George, as we departed. "I'm glad you came, Mr. Ticehurst, for I'm off too quick."

As we rode back to Thomson Forks, Harmer asked pathetically what he was to do.

"We must see, Jack," I answered kindly. "We'll get you something in town."

"I'd rather be with you," he answered dolorously.

"Well, you can't yet, that's certain," said I. "I can't afford to pay you wages, when there will be no more than I can get through myself; when there is, I'll let you know. In the meantime you must make money, Jack. There's a sawmill in town. I know the man that runs it—Bill Custer, and I'll go and see him for you."

Jack sighed, and we rode on in silence until we reached the Forks.

After we had had supper Jack and I were standing in the barroom, not near the stove, which was surrounded by a small crowd of men, who smoked and chewed and chattered, but close by the door for the sake of the fresher air, when we saw Siwash Jim ride up. After tying his horse to the rail in front of the house, to which half a dozen other animals in various stages of equine despondency or irritation were already attached, he swaggered into the bar, brushing against me rather rudely as he did so. Harmer's eyes flashed with indignation, as if it was he who had been insulted. But I am a very peaceable man, and don't always fight at the first chance. Besides, being so much bigger than Jim, I could, I considered, afford to take no notice of what an ill-conditioned little ruffian like that did when he was probably drunk. Presently Jack spoke to me.

"That beastly fellow keeps looking at you, Mr. Ticehurst, as if he would like to cut your throat. What's wrong with him? Is he jealous of you, do you think?"

It was almost blasphemy to dream of such a thing, and I looked at Mr.

John Harmer so sternly that he apologized; yet I believe it must to some extent have been that which caused the trouble that ensued almost directly, and added afterward to the danger in which I already stood. I turned round and looked at Jim, who returned my glance furiously. He ordered another drink, and then another. It seemed as if he was desirous of making himself drunk. Presently Dave, who was, as usual, behind the bar, spoke to him.

"Going back to the ranch to-night, Jim?"

Jim struck the bar hard with his fist.

"No, I'm not! Never, unless I go to set the damned place on fire!"

"Why, what's the matter?" asked Dave, smiling, while Harmer and I pricked up our ears.

"Ah! I had some trouble with old Fleming just now," said Jim, in a hoarse voice of passion. "He's like the rest, wants too much; the more one does, the more one may do. He's a dirty coyote, and his girls are——" And the gentle-minded Jim used an epithet which made both our ears tingle.

Jack made a spring, but I caught him by the shoulder and sent him spinning back, and walked up alongside the men. I saw my own face in the glass at the back of the bar; it was very white, and I could hardly recognize it.

"Mind what you say, you infernal ruffian!" I said, in a low voice, "or I'll break your neck for you! Don't you dare to speak about ladies, you dog, or I'll strangle you!" He sprang back like lightning. If he had had a six-shooter on him I think my story would have ended here, for I had none myself. But Jim had no weapon. Yet he was no coward, and did not "take water," or "back down," as they say there. He steadied himself one moment, and then threw the water-bottle at me with all his force. Though I ducked, I did not quite escape it, for the handle caught me on the forehead near the hair, and, in breaking, cut a gash which sent the blood down into my left eye. But I caught hold of him before he could do anything else. In a moment the room was in an uproar; some of the men climbed on to the tables in order to get a view, while those outside crowded to the door. They roared, "Leave 'em alone!" when Dave attempted to approach, and one big fellow caught hold of Harmer and held him, saying at the same time, as Jack told me afterward, "You stay right here, sonny, and see 'em fight. Mebbe you'll larn something!"

I found Jim a much tougher customer than I should have imagined, although I might have handled him more easily if I had not been for the time blind in one eye. But he was like a bunch of muscle; his arms, though slender, were as tough and hard as his stock-whip handle, and his quickness was surprising. He struck me once or twice as we grappled, and then we fell, rolling over and over, and scattering the onlookers, as we went, until we came against the legs of the table, which gave way and sent three men to the floor with a shock that shook the house. Finally, Jim got his hand in my hair and tried to gouge out my eyes. Fortunately, it was not long enough for him to get a good hold, but when I felt his thumbs feeling for my eyes, all the strength and rage I ever had seemed to come to me, and I rose suddenly with him clinging to me. For a moment we swayed about, and then I caught his throat, pushed him at arm's length from me, and, catching hold of his belt, I threw him right over my head. I was standing with my back to the door, and he went through it, fell on the sidewalk, and rolled off into the road, where he lay insensible.

"Very good!" said Dave; "very well done indeed! Pick him up, some of you fellows, and see if he's dead. The son of a gun, I'll make him pay for that bottle, and for the table! Come, have a drink, Mr. Ticehurst. You look rather warm."

I should think I did, besides being smothered with blood and dust. I was glad to accept his invitation.

"Is he dead?" I asked of Harmer, who came in just then.

"Not he," said Jack, "he's coming to already, but I guess he'll fight no more for a few days. That must have been a sickener. By Jove! how strong you must be—he went out of the door like a stone out of a sling. Lucky he didn't hit the post." And Harmer chuckled loudly, and then went off with me to wash away the blood, and bandage the cut in my forehead.

When I left town in the morning I heard that Jim was still in bed and likely to stay there for some time. And Harmer, who was going to work with Bill Custer, promised to let me know if he heard anything which was of importance to me.

On my way out to my new property I met its late owner and his Indian wife in their ricketty wagon, drawn by the horse I had not thought worth buying. Nettlebury was more than half drunk, although it was early in the morning, and when he saw me coming he rose up, waved his hand to me, bellowed, "I'm a-goin' East, I am!" and, falling over the seat backward, disappeared from view. Alice reached out her hand and helped her husband to regain his former position. I came up alongside and reined in my horse.

He looked at me.

"Been fightin' already, hev you; or did you get chucked off? More likely you got chucked—it takes an American to ride these cay uses!" said he half scornfully.

"No," said I, "I wasn't chucked, and I have been fighting. Did you hear why Siwash Jim left Fleming!"

"No, not exactly," he returned; "but he was sassy with Miss Elsie, and—oh, I dunno—but you hev been fightin', eh? Did you lick him—and who was it?"

"The man himself, Mr. Nettlebury," said I—"Jim; and I reckon I did whip him."

He laughed.

"Good on you, old man! He's been wanting it this long while past; but look out he don't put a knife in your ribs. Now then," said he ferociously, turning to his wife, "why don't you drive on? Here, catch hold!" and giving her the reins, he lifted his hand to strike her. But just then the old horse started up, he fell over the seat again, and lay there on a pile of sacking. I hardly thought he would get East with his money, and I was right, for I hired him to work for me soon afterward.

When I came to the Flemings' there was no one about but the old man.

"Busy!" said he, "you may bet I'm busy. I sent that black ruffian off yesterday, and I've got no one to help me. What's the matter with your head?"

When I told him, he laughed heartily, and then shook my hand.

"I'm glad you thrashed him, Tom," said he; "I'd have done it myself yesterday if I had been ten years younger. When Elsie wanted him to get some water, he growled and said all klootchmen, as he calls 'em—women, you know—were alike, Indian or white, and no good. I told him to get out. Is he badly hurt?"

"Not very," I answered.

"I hoped he was," said the old man. "It's a pity you didn't break his neck! I would as soon trust a black snake! Are you going over yonder?"

"I guess so," I answered; "I must get the place cleaned up a bit—it's like a pigsty, or what they call a hog-pen in this country,"

"Well, I guess it is," he replied; "but come over in the evening, if you like."

I thanked him and rode off, happy in one thing at least—I was near Elsie. I felt as if Harmer's suspicions about Mat were a mere chimera, and that the lad in some excitement had mistaken the dark face of some harmless Indian for that of the revengeful Malay. And as to Siwash Jim, why, I shrugged my shoulders; I did not suppose he was so murderously inclined as Nettlebury imagined. It would be hard lines on me to have two men so ill disposed toward me, through no fault of my own, as to wish to kill me.

I went back to the Flemings' after a hard day's work, in which I burnt, or otherwise disposed of, an almost unparalleled collection of rubbish, including old crockery and bottles, dirty shirts and worn-out boots, which had been accumulating indoors and out for some ten years. After being nearly smothered, I was glad to go down to the creek and take a bath in the clear, cold water which ran into the main watercourse issuing, some two miles away, from the Black Cañon at the back of the valley, concerning which Fleming had once spoken to me. That evening at his ranch was the pleasantest I ever spent in my life up to that time, in spite of the black cloud which hung over me, for Fanny was as bright and happy as a bird, while Elsie, who seemed to have come to her senses, spoke almost freely, displaying no more disinclination to me, even apparently, than might naturally be set down to her instinctive modesty, and her knowledge that I was courting her, and desired to be received as her lover.

I spoke to her late that evening when Fleming went out to throw down the night's hay to his horses. For Fanny vanished discreetly at the same moment, and continued to make just enough noise in the kitchen to assure us she was there, while it was not sufficient to drown even the softest conversation. Good girl she was, and is—I love her yet, though—well, perhaps I had better leave that unsaid at present.

"Elsie," I said, when we were alone, "do you remember what I said when we parted on the steamer?"

She cast her eyes down, but did not answer.

"I think you do, Elsie," I went on; "I said I should never forget. Do you think I have? Don't you know why I left my ship, why I came to this country, why I went mining, and why I have worked so hard and patiently for long, long months without seeing you? Answer me; do you know why?"

She hesitated a moment, lifted up her blue eyes, dropped them at the sight of the passion in mine, and said gently, "I suppose so, Mr. Ticehurst."

"Yes, you know, Elsie; it was that I might be near you, that I might get rich enough to be able to claim you. How fortunate I have been in that! But am I fortunate in other things, too, Elsie? Will you answer me that, Elsie?"

I approached her, but she held up her hand.

"Stay, Mr. Ticehurst!—if I must speak. I may have judged you wrongly, but I am not wholly sure that I have. If I have not, I should only be preparing misery for myself and for you, if I answered your questions as you would have me. I want time, and I must have it, or some other assurance; for how can I wholly trust you when you will not speak as you might do?"

Ah! how could I? But this was far better than I had expected—far better.

"Elsie," I answered quietly, "I am ready to give you time, all the time you need to prove me, and my love for you, though there is no need. My heart is yours, and yours only, ever from the time I saw you. I have never even wavered in my faith and hope. But I do not care so long as I may be near you—so long as I may see you sometimes, and speak to you. For without you I shall be wretched, and would be glad even if that wretched Malay were to kill me, as he threatened."

I thought I was cunning to bring in Matthias, and indeed she lifted her eyes then. But she showed no signs of fear for me. Perhaps she looked at me, saying to herself there was no need of such a strong man being afraid of such a visionary danger. She spoke after a little silence.

"Then let it be so, Mr. Ticehurst. If what you say be true, there at least is nothing for you to fear."

She looked at me straight then with her glorious blue eyes, and I would have given worlds to catch her in my arms and press her to my heart. She went on:

"And if you never give me cause, why—" She was silent, but held out her hand.

I took it, pressed it, and would have raised it to my lips, only she drew it gently away. But I went to rest happy that night. Give her cause!—indeed, what cause could I give her? That is what I asked myself, without knowing what was coming, without feeling my ignorance, my blindness, and my helplessness in the strange web of fate and fated crime which was being woven around me—without being conscious, as an animal is in the prairie, of that storm, so ready to burst on my head, whose first faint clouds had risen on the horizon of my life, even before I had seen her, in the very hour that I had joined the *Vancouver* under my own brother's command. I went to sleep, wondering vaguely what had become of him. But we are blind, all of us, and see nothing until the curtain rises on act after act; being ignorant still, whether the end shall be sweet or bitter to us, whether it shall justify our smiles in happiness, or our tears in some bitter tragedy.

For two days I worked in and about my house, putting things in some order, and on the third I rode over to the Flemings' early in the morning, as it had been arranged that I was to go out with Mr. Fleming to look after some cattle of his, which a neighbor had complained of. I never felt in better spirits than when I rode over the short two miles which separated us, for the morning was calm and bright, with a touch of that glorious freshness known only among mountains or on high plateaus lifted up from the common level of the under world. I even sang softly to myself, for the black cloud of doubt, which but a few days ago had obscured all my light, was driven away by a new dawning of hope, and I was content and without fear. I shouted cheerfully for Fleming as I rode up, and he came to the door with his whip over his arm, followed by the two girls. I alighted, and shook hands all round.

"Then you are ready, Mr. Fleming?" I asked.

"When I have put the saddle on the black horse," he replied, as he went toward the stable, leaving me standing there, for I was little inclined to offer to assist him while Elsie remained outside the house. Fanny was quite as mischievous as ever, and whether her sister had told her anything of what had passed between us two days before or not, she was evidently conscious that the relations between Elsie and myself had somehow altered for the better.

"How do you find yourself these days, Tom?" she asked, with a merry twinkle in her eye.

"Very well, Fanny," I answered. "Thanks for your inquiry."

"Does the climate suit you, then? Or is it the surroundings?"

"Both, my dear girl, as long as the sun shines on us!" I replied, laughing, while Elsie turned away with a smile.

Fanny almost winked at me, and then looked up the road toward Thomson Forks, which ran close by the ranch and led toward an Indian settlement on the Lake about ten miles away.

"There's someone coming," she said, "and he's in a hurry. Isn't he galloping, Mr. Ticehurst?"

I looked up the road and saw somebody who certainly was coming down the long slope from the crest of the hill with more than reasonable rapidity. I looked, and then turned away carelessly. What was the horseman to me? I leant against the post of the veranda, which some former occupant of the house had ornamented by whittling with his knife, until it was almost too thin to do its duty, and began to speak to Fanny again, when I saw her blush and start.

"Why, Mr. Ticehurst," she said, "it's Mr. Harmer!"

Then the horseman was something to me, after all. For what but some urgent need would bring Jack, who was entirely ignorant of horses and riding, at that breakneck gallop over the mountain road? My carelessness went suddenly, and I felt my heart begin to beat with unaccustomed violence. I turned pale, I know, as I watched him coming nearer. I was quite unconscious that Elsie had rejoined her sister, and stood behind me.

Harmer came closer and closer, and when he saw us waved his hat. In a moment he was at the gate, while I stood still at the house, and did not move to go toward him. He alighted, opened the gate, and, with his bridle over his aim, came up to us. He said good-morning to the girls hurriedly, and turned to me.

"You must come to Thomson Forks directly, Mr. Ticehurst!" he said, gasping, wiping his forehead with his sleeve. "Something's happened, I don't know what, and I can't tell; but she wants to see you at once, and sent me off to fetch you—and so I came, and, oh! how sore I am," and he wriggled suggestively, and in a way that would have been comic under other circumstances.

I caught hold of his arm.

"What do you mean," I roared, "you young fool? What's happened, and who wants to see me? Who's *she*?"

He looked up in astonishment.

"Why, didn't I say Mrs. Ticehurst, of course?"

I let him go and fell against the post, making it crack as I did so. I looked at Elsie, and she was white and stern. But she did not avoid my eye.

"Well, what is it—what's happened?" I said at last.

"I don't know, I tell you, sir," said he almost piteously; "all I know is that I was sent for to the sawmill by Dave, and when I came I saw Mrs. Ticehurst; and she's dressed in black, sir, and she looked dreadfully bad, and she just shook hands with me, and told me to fetch you at once. And when I asked what for, she just stamped, sir, and told me to go. And so I came, and that's all!"

Surely it was enough. Much as I liked her, I would rather have met Mat or the very devil in the way than had this happen now, when things were going so well with me. And in black?—good God! had anything happened to my brother? I turned white, I know, and almost fell.

"You had better go at once, Tom," laid Fanny, who held me by the arm. I turned, I hardly know why, to her sister. Her face was very pale, but her eyes glittered, and she looked like marble. I know my own asked hers a question, but I got no response. I turned away toward my horse, and then she spoke.

"Mr. Ticehurst, let me speak to you one moment. Fanny, go and talk to Mr. Harmer."

And Fanny and I both obeyed her like children.

She looked at me straight.

"How could I prove you, Mr. Ticehurst," she said, in a low voice, "was what I asked the other night. Now the means are in my power. What are you going to do?"

"I am going to the Forks," I said, in bewilderment. Her eyes flashed, and she looked at me scornfully.

"Then go, but don't ever speak to me again! Go!"

And she turned away. I caught her arm.

"Don't be unjust, Elsie!—don't be cruelly unjust!" I cried. What a fool I was; I knew she loved me, and yet I asked her not to be cruel and unjust. Can a woman or a man in love be anything else?

"How can I stay away?" I asked passionately, "when my brother's wife sends for me? And she is in black—poor Will must be dead!"

If he was dead, then Helen was free. I saw that and so did Elsie, and it hardened her more than ever, for she did not answer.

"Look then, Elsie, I am going, and you say I shall not speak to you again. You are cruel, very cruel—but I love you! And you shall speak to me—aye, and one day ask my pardon for doubting me. But even for you I cannot refuse this request of my own sister-in-law—who is ill, alone, in sorrow and trouble, in a strange land. For the present, good-by!"

I turned away, took my horse from the fence, and rode off rapidly, without thinking of Harmer, or of Fleming, who was standing in amazement at his stable, as I saw when I opened the swing-gate. And if Harmer had come up at a gallop, I went at one, until my horse was covered with sweat, and the foam, flying from his champed bit, hung about my knees like sea-foam that did not easily melt. In half an hour I was at Conlan's door, and was received by Dave. In two minutes I stood in Helen's presence.

When I saw her last she had that rich red complexion which showed the pure color of the blood through a delicate skin; her eyes were piercing and perhaps a little hard, and her figure was full and beautiful. She had always rejoiced, too, in bright colors, such as an Oriental might have chosen, and their richness had suited her striking appearance. But now she was woefully altered, and I barely knew her. The color had deserted her cheeks, which were wan and hollow; her eyes were sunken and ringed with dark circles, and her bust had fallen in until she looked like the ghost of her former self, a ghost that was but a mere vague memory of her whom I had first known in Melbourne.

Her dress, too, was black, which I knew she hated, and in which she looked even less like herself. Her voice, when she spoke, no longer rang out with assurance, but faltered ever and again with the tears that rose to her eyes and checked her utterance.

I took her hand, full of pity for her, and dread of what she had to tell me, for it must be something dreadful which had changed her so much and brought her so far.

"What is it, Helen?" I said, in a low voice.

"What did I come for, you mean, Tom?" she asked, though desiring no answer. "I came for your sake—and not for Will's. I thought you might never get a letter, and I wanted to see you once again. Ah! how much I desired that. Tom, you are in danger!" she spoke that suddenly—"in danger every moment! For that man who threatened your life——"

I nodded, sucking my dry lips, for I knew what she meant, and I was only afraid of what else she had to tell me.

"That man has escaped, and has not been caught. O Tom, be careful—be careful! If you were to die, too——"

"What do you mean, Helen?" I asked, though I knew full well what she meant. She looked at me.

"Can't you think? Yes, you can perhaps partly; but not all—not all the horror of it. Tom, Will is dead! And not only that, but he was murdered in San Francisco!"

I staggered, and sat down staring at her. She went on in a curiously constrained voice.

"Yes; the very first night we came ashore, and in our hotel! He was intoxicated, and came in late, and I wouldn't have him in my room. I made them put him in the next, and I heard him shouting out of his window over the veranda soon afterward, and then I fell asleep. And in the morning I found him—I myself found him dead in bed, struck right through with a stab in the heart. And he was robbed, too. Tom, it nearly killed me, it was so horrible—oh, it was horrible! I didn't know what to do. I was going to send for you, and then I read in the paper about Mat having escaped two days before, so I came away at once."

She ceased and sobbed violently; and I kept silence. God alone knows what was in my heart, and how it came there; but for a moment—yes, and for more than that—I suspected her, his wife, of my brother's murder! I was blind enough, I suppose, and so was she; but then so many times in life we wonder suddenly at our want of sight when the truth comes out. I remembered she had once said she hated him, and could kill him. And besides, she loved me. I shivered and was still silent. She looked up and caught my eye, which, I knew, was full of doubt. She rose up suddenly, came to me, fell on her knees, and cried:

"No, no, Tom—not that! For God's sake, don't look at me so!"

And I knew she saw my very heart, and I was ashamed of myself. I lifted her up and put her on a chair. Heavens! how light she was to what she had been, for her soul had wasted her body away like a strong wind fanning a fire.

"Poor Will!" I said at last, and then I asked if she had remained for the inquest. No, she had not, she answered. I started at her reply. If I could think what I had, what might others not do? For her to disappear like that after the murder of her husband was enough to make people believe her guilty of the crime, and I wondered that she had not been prevented from leaving. But on questioning her further, I learnt that the police suspected a certain man who was a frequenter of that very hotel; and, after the manner of their kind, had got him in custody, and were devoting all their attention to proving him guilty of the crime, whether there were *prima facie* proofs or not. Still, it seemed bitter that poor Will should be left to strangers while his wife came to see me; and though she had done it to save me, as she thought, yet, after all, the danger was hardly such as to warrant her acting as she had done. But I was not the person to blame her. She had done it, poor woman, because she yet loved me, as I knew even then. But I saw, too, that it was love without hope; and even if it had not been, she must have learnt that I was near to Elsie; and that I was "courting old Fleming's gal" was the common talk whenever my name was mentioned. I tried to convince myself that she had most likely ceased to think of me, and I preferred to believe it was only the daily and hourly irritation of poor Will's conduct which had driven her to compare me with him to his disadvantage. Well, whatever his faults were, they had been bitterly expiated; as, indeed, such faults as his usually are. It does not require statistics to convince anyone who has seen much of the world that most of the trouble in it comes directly from drink.

I was in a strange situation as I sat reflecting. I suppose strict duty required me to go to San Francisco, and yet Will would be buried before I could get there. Then what was I to do with his widow? She could not stay there, I could not allow it, nor did I think she desired it. Still she was not fit to travel in her state of nervous exhaustion; indeed, it was a marvel that she had been able to come so far, even under the stimulus of such unwonted excitement. I could not go away with her even for a part of the return journey, for I felt Elsie would be harder and harder to manage the more she knew I saw of Helen. I ended by coming to the conclusion that she must stay at the Forks for a while, and that I must go back and try to have an explanation with Elsie. Helen bowed her head in acquiescence when I told her what she had better do, for the poor woman was utterly broken down, and ready to lean on any arm that was offered her; and she, who had been so strong in her own will, was at last content to be advised like an obedient child. I left her with Mrs. Conlan, to whom I told as much as I thought desirable, and, kissing her on the forehead, I took my horse and rode slowly toward home.

As I left the town I saw Siwash Jim sitting on the sidewalk, and he looked at me with a face full of diabolical hatred. When I got to the crest of the hill above the town I turned in the saddle, and saw him still gazing after me.

When half-way home I met Harmer, who was riding even slower than I, and sitting as gingerly in the saddle as if he were very uncomfortable, as I had no doubt he was.

"Well, Mr. Ticehurst," said he eagerly, when we came near, "what was it?"

I told him, and he looked puzzled.

"Well," he remarked at last, "it seems to me I must have been mistaken after all, and that I didn't see Mat when I thought I did. Let me see, when did he escape?"

I reckoned it up, and it was only twelve days ago, for Helen had taken nine days coming from San Francisco, according to what she told me.

"Then it is impossible for me to have seen him in New Westminster," said Harmer. "But it is very strange that I should have imagined I did see him, and that he did escape after all."

Then I told him of my brother's death.

"Why, Mr. Ticehurst," he exclaimed, "Matthias must have done it himself! He must—don't you see he must?"

The thought had not entered into my head.

"No," said I; "I don't see it at all. There's a man in custody for it now, and it is hardly likely Mat would stay in San Francisco, if he escaped, for two days. Besides, it is even less likely that he would fall across my brother the very first evening he came ashore."

Harmer shook his head obstinately.

"We shall see, sir—we shall see. You know he didn't like Captain Ticehurst much better than you. Then, you say he was robbed of his papers. Was your address among them, do you think?"

I started, for Jack's suspicion seemed possible after all. The thing, looked more likely than it had done at first sight. And yet it was only my cowardice that made me think so. I shook my head, but answered "yes" to his question.

"Then pray, Mr. Ticehurst, be careful," said Jack earnestly, "and carry your revolver always. Besides, that fellow Jim is about again. You hardly hurt him at all; he must be made of iron, and I heard last night he threatened to have your life."

"Threatened men live long, Jack," said I. "I am not scared of him. That's only talk and blow. I don't care much if Mat doesn't get on my track. He would be dangerous. Did you see Miss Fleming before you left?" I said, turning the conversation.

He shook his head. She had gone to her room, and remained there when I went away.

"Well, Harmer, I shall be in town the day after to-morrow," I said at last, "and if anything happens, you can send me word; and go and see Mrs. Ticehurst meanwhile."

"I will do that," said he, "but to-morrow morning I have to go up the lake to the logging camp, and don't know when I shall be back. That's what Custer said this morning, when I asked him to let me come over here."

"Very well, it won't matter, I dare say," I answered. "Take care of yourself, Jack."

"Oh, Mr. Ticehurst," said he, turning round in the saddle, and wincing as he did so, "it is you who must be careful! Pray, do be very careful!"

I nodded, shook hands, and rode on.

When I came to the Flemings', Fanny was at the big gate, and she asked a question by her eyes before we got close enough to speak.

"Yes, Fanny," said I, "it was serious." And then I told her what had occurred. She held out her hand and pressed mine sympathetically.

"I am so sorry, Tom," was all she said; but she said it so kindly that her voice almost brought the tears to my eyes.

"Has Elsie spoken to you since I went, Fanny?" I asked, as we walked down to the house together, while my horse followed with his head hanging down.

"I haven't even seen her, Tom," she replied; "the door was locked, and when I knocked she told me to go away, which, as it's my room too, was not very polite."

In spite of my love for Elsie, I felt somewhat bitter against her injustice to me, and I was glad to see that I made her suffer a little on her part. I know I have said very little about my own feelings, for I don't care somehow to put down all that I felt, any more than I like to tell any stranger all that is near my heart; but I did feel strongly and deeply, and to see her, who was with me by day and night as the object of my fondest hope, so unjust, was enough to make me bitter. I wished to reproach her, for I was not a child—a boy, to be fooled with like this.

"Go and ask her to see me, Fanny, please," I said rather sternly, as I stood outside the door. "And don't tell her anything of what I told you, either of Will or Matthias."

Fanny started.

"You never said anything of Matthias!" she cried.

"Didn't I, Fanny? Well, then, I will. He has escaped from prison, and I suppose he is after me by this. But don't tell Elsie. Just say I want to see her."

In a few moments she came back, with tears in her eyes.

"She won't, Tom! She is in an obstinate fit, I know. And though she is crying her eyes out—the spiteful cat!—she won't come. I know her. She just told me to go away. What shall I do?" she asked.

"Nothing, Fanny," I answered; "you can tell her what you like. Will you be so cruel to your lover, little Fanny?"

She looked up saucily.

"I don't know, Tom; I shall see when I have one"—and she laughed.

"What about Jack Harmer, then?"

"Well, you see," and she looked down, "he's very young." She wasn't more than seventeen herself, and looked younger. "And, besides, I don't care for anybody but Elsie and father and you, Tom."

"Very well, Fanny," said I; "give me a kiss from Elsie, and make her give it you back."

"I will, Tom," she said quite simply, and, kissing her, I rode off quietly across the flat to my solitary home.

PART V AT THE BLACK CAÑON.

Now, as far as I have gone in this story, I have related nothing which I did not see or hear myself, which is, as it seems to me, the proper way to do it, provided nothing important is left out. But as I have learnt since then what happened to other people, and have pieced the story together in my mind, I see it is necessary to depart from the rule I have observed hitherto, if I don't want to explain, after I have come to the end of the whole history, what occurred before; and that, I can see, would be a very clumsy way of narrating any affair. Now, what I am going to tell I have on very good evidence, for Dave at the Forks, and Conlan's stableman told me part, and afterward, as will be seen, I actually learnt something from Siwash Jim himself, who here plays rather a curious and important part.

It appears that the day after I was at the Forks (which day I spent, by the way, with Mr. Fleming, riding round the country, returning afterward by the trail which led from the Black Cañon down to my house) Siwash Jim, who had to all appearance recovered from the injuries, which, however, were only bruises, that I had inflicted on him, began to drink early in the morning. He had, so Dave says, quite an unnatural power of keeping sober—and Dave himself can drink more than any two men I am acquainted with, unless it is Mac, my old partner, so he ought to know. And though Jim drank hard, he did not become drunk, but only abused me. He called me all the names from coyote upward and downward which a British Columbian of any standing has at his tongue's end, and when Jim had exhausted the resources of the fertile American language, he started in Siwash or Indian, in which there are many choice terms of abuse. But in spite of his openness, Dave says it was quite evident he was dangerous, and that I might really have been in peril at any time of the day if I had come to town, for Jim was deemed a bad character among his companions, and had, so it was said, killed one man at least, though he had never been tried for it. But though he sat all day in the bar, using my name openly, he never made a move till eight in the evening, when he went out for awhile.

When he returned he was accompanied by a thin dark man, wearing a slouch hat over his eyes, whom Dave took to be a half-breed of some kind, and they had drinks together, for which the stranger paid, speaking in good English, but not with a Western accent. Then the two went to the other side of the room. What their conversation was, no one knows exactly, nor did I ever learn; but Dave, who was keeping his eye on Jim, says that it seemed as if the stranger was trying to persuade Jim to be quiet and stay where he was, and from what occurred afterward there is little doubt his supposition was correct. Moreover, my name undoubtedly occurred in this conversation, for Dave heard it, and the name of my ranch as well. Soon after that some men came in, and, in consequence of his being busy, Dave did not see Jim go out. But Conlan's stableman says Jim came to the stable with the stranger and got his horse. When asked where he was going, he said for a ride, and would answer no more questions. And all the time the strange man tried to persuade him not to go, and to come and have another drink. If Jim had been flush of money there might have been a motive for this, but as he was not, there seemed then to be none beyond the sudden and absurd fondness that men sometimes conceive for each other when drunk. But if this were the case, it was only on the stranger's side, for when the horse was brought round to the door Jim mounted it, and when the other man still importuned him not to go, Siwash Jim struck at him with his left hand and knocked off his hat as he stood in the light coming from the bar. And just then attention was drawn from Jim by a sudden shriek from the other side of the road where Conlan's private house stood. When Dave came out and looked for him again, both he and the other man had disappeared down the road, which branched about half a mile out of town into two forks, one leading eastward and the other southward to the Flemings'.

Now, as I said before, most of that day I had been out riding with Mr. Fleming, who left me early, in order to go to the next ranch down the road, and I had told him the whole story about Mat's escape, and my brother's death; which he agreed with me were hardly likely to be connected. Yet he acknowledged if they were I was in much more danger than one would have thought before, because such a deed would show the Malay was a desperado of the most fearless and dangerous description; and besides, if he had robbed Will, it was more than likely he knew where I was from my own letters, or from my address written in a pocketbook my brother always carried, and which was missing. Of course, this conversation made me full, as it were, of Mat; and that, combined with the unlucky turn affairs had taken with regard to Elsie, made me more nervous than I was inclined to acknowledge to her father. So before I went to bed, which I did at ten o'clock—for I was very tired, being still unaccustomed to much riding—I locked my door carefully, and put the table against it, neither of which things I had ever done before, and which I was almost inclined to undo at once, for it seemed cowardly to me. Yet I thought of Elsie, and, still hoping to win her, I was careful of my life. I went to sleep, in spite of my nervous preoccupation, almost as soon as I lay down, and I suppose I must have been asleep two hours before I woke out of a horrible dream. I thought that I was on board ship, in my own berth, lying in the bunk, and that Mat was on my chest strangling me with his long lithe fingers. And all the time I heard, as I thought, the sails flap, as though the vessel had come up in the wind. As I struggled—and I did struggle desperately—the blood seemed to go up into my head and eyes, until I saw the fiend's face in a red light, and then I woke. The house was on fire, and I was being suffocated! As the flames worked in from the outside, and made the scorching timbers crack again and again, I sprang out of bed. I had lain down with my trousers on, and, seeing at once there must be foul play for the house to catch fire on the outside, and at the back too, where I never went, I drew on my boots, snatched my revolver up, and leapt at the front window, through which I went with a crash, uttering a loud cry as I did so, for a piece of the glass cut my left arm deeply. As I came to the ground, I saw a horseman in front of me, and by the light of the fire, which had already mounted to the roof of the house, I recognized Siwash Jim. Then, whether it was that the horse he rode was frightened at the crash I made or not, it suddenly bounded into the air, turned sharp round, and bolted into the brush, just where the trail came down from the Black Cañon. As Jim disappeared, I fired, but with no effect; and that my shot was neither returned nor anticipated was, I saw, due to the fact that the villain had dropped his own six-shooter, probably at the first bound of his horse, just where he had been standing.

I was in a blind fury of rage, for such a cowardly and treacherous attack on an unoffending man's life seemed hardly credible to me. And there my home was burning, and it was no fault of his that I was not burning with it, or shot dead outside my own door. But he should not escape, if I chased him for a month. I was glad he had been forced to take the trail, for there was no possible outlet to it for miles, so thick was the brush in that mountainous region. Fortunately, I now had two horses; and the one in my stable, which I had only bought from Fleming a week before, was not the one I had been riding all that day. I threw the saddle on him, clinched it up tightly, and led him out. I carried both the weapons, my own and Jim's, and I rode up the narrow and winding path in a blind and desperate fury, which seldom comes to a man, but it when it does it makes him careless of his own life and utterly reckless; and as I rode, in a fashion I had never done before, even though I trusted a mountain-bred and forest-trained horse, I swore that I myself should die that night, or that Siwash Jim should feel the just weight of my wrath. But before I can tell the terrible story of that terrible night I must return once more, and for the last time, to Thomson Forks.

I said, some pages back, that attention had been drawn from Siwash Jim and his strange companion by a sudden shriek from Ned Conlan's house. That shriek had been uttered by Helen, who was still staying with Mrs. Conlan, as she and her hostess were standing outside in the dying twilight, and, after screaming, she had fainted, remaining insensible for nearly half an hour. When Dr. Smith, as he called himself—though an Englishman has natural doubts as to how the practitioners in the West earn their diplomas—had helped her recovery, she spoke at once in a state of nervous excitement painful to witness.

"Oh, I saw him—I saw him!" she said, in an hysterical voice.

"Who, my dear?" asked Mrs. Conlan, in what people call a comforting way.

"Where is Mr Conlan?" was Helen's answer. He came into the room in which she was lying. Helen turned to him at once.

"Mr. Conlan, I want you to take me out to my brother-in-law's house—to Mr. Ticehurst's farm!"

They all exclaimed against her foolishness and demanded why; while Conlan scratched his head in a puzzled manner.

"I tell you I must see him to-night, and at once! For I saw the man who swore to kill him."

The bystanders shook their heads sagely, thinking she was mad, but Conlan asked if she meant Siwash Jim.

"No," she said, "it was not Jim." But she must go, and she would. With an extraordinary exhibition of strength, she rose and ordered horses in an imperative tone, saying she was quite well enough to do as she liked.

Mrs. Conlan appealed to the doctor, and he, perhaps being glad to advise against the opinion of those present, as such a course might indicate his superior knowledge, said he thought it best to let her have her own way. I think, too, that Helen, who seemed to have regained her strength, had regained with it her old power of making people do as she wished. At any rate, Mr. Conlan meekly acquiesced, and, saying he would drive her himself, went out to order horses at once. When the buggy was brought to the door, Helen got up without assistance, and begged him to be quick. His wife, who would never have dared to even suggest his hurrying, stood aghast at seeing her usually masterful husband do as he was bid. They drove off, leaving Mrs. Conlan to prophesy certain death as the result of this inexplicable expedition, while the others speculated, more or less wildly, as to what it all meant.

Conlan told me that Helen never spoke all the way except to ask how much longer they were going to be, or to complain of the slowness of the pace.

"Most women," said Ned, "would have been scared at the way I drove, for it was pitch dark; and if the horses hadn't known the road as well, or better, than I did, we should have come to grief in the first mile. But she never turned a hair. She was a wonderful woman, sir!"

It was already past eleven o'clock when they got to the top of the hill just above Fleming's, and from there the light of my house burning could be distinctly seen, although the place itself was hidden by a rise, and Helen pointed to it, nervously demanding what it was.

"Ticehurst must have been burning brush," said Conlan, offering the very likeliest explanation. But Helen said, "No, no," impatiently, and told him to hurry. Just then Conlan remembered that he did not know the road across from Fleming's to my place, and said so.

"You had better stop at Fleming's, and send for him. They aint in bed yet, ma'am. I see their light."

"I don't want to see the Flemings; I want Mr. Ticehurst," said Helen obstinately.

"Well, we must stop at Fleming's," said Conlan, "if it's only to ask the way. I don't know the road, and I'm not going to kill you and myself by driving into the creek such a night as this."

And Helen was fain to acquiesce, for she could not do otherwise.

When they reached the house Fanny was standing outside, and as the light from the open door fell on Helen's pallid face, she screamed.

"Good Heavens, Mrs. Ticehurst! Is it you?" she cried—"and you, Mr. Conlan? Oh, I am so glad!—father's away, and Mr. Ticehurst's house must be on fire."

"Ah!" said Helen, "I thought so. Oh, oh! he's dead, I know he's dead! I must go to him! Fanny, dear, can you show us the way—can you? You must! Perhaps we can save him yet!"

She frightened Fanny terribly, for her face was so pale and her eyes glittered so, and for a moment the girl could hardly speak.

"I don't know it by night, Mrs. Ticehurst; but Elsie does," she said at last.

"Where is she, then?" said Helen eagerly.

"She's gone over there now," cried Fanny, "for father had not come home; and when we saw the fire, we were afraid something had happened, so Elsie took the black horse and went over. She's there now."

"Then what shall we do?" cried Helen, in an agony, "he will be killed!"

"What is it, Mrs. Ticehurst?" asked Fanny, trembling all over. "Oh, what is it!"

But she took no notice and sat like a statue, only she breathed hard and heavily, and her hands twitched; as she looked toward my burning home.

"Silence!" she cried suddenly, though no one spoke. "There is somebody coming."

And the three of them looked into the darkness, in which there was a white figure moving rapidly.

"It is Elsie!" screamed Fanny joyfully; and Helen sprang from the buggy, and stood in the light, as Elsie exclaimed in wonder at Fanny's excited voice.

The two women stood face to face, looking in each other's eyes, and then Elsie, who for one moment had shown nothing but surprise, went white with scorn and anger. How glad I should have been to have seen her so, or to have learnt, even at that moment when I stood in the greatest peril I have ever known, that she had ridden over to save or help me, even though her acts but added a greater danger to those in which I already stood. For her deed and her look were the deed and look of a woman who loves and is jealous. But it might have seemed to me, had I been there, that Helen's coming had overbalanced the scale once more against me, and perhaps for the last time. I am glad I did not know that fear until it was only imagination, and the imaginary canceling of a series of events, that could place me again in such a situation.

The two women looked at each other, and then Elsie turned away.

"Stop, stop!" cried Helen; "what has happened? Where is Mr. Ticehurst?"

"What is that to you?" said Elsie cruelly, and with her eyes flaming.

"Tell us, Elsie," said Fanny imploringly.

"I will *not*!" said her sister—"not to this woman! Go back, Mrs. Ticehurst! What are you doing here?"

Helen caught her by the arm, and looked in her face.

"Girl, I know your thoughts!" she said; "but you are wrong—I tell you, you are wrong! You love him——"

"I do not!" said Elsie angrily. "I love no other woman's lover!"

Surely, though there were two dazed onlookers, these women were in a state to speak their natural minds.

"Girl, girl!" said Helen, once more, "I tell you again, you are wrong! You are endangering *your* lover's life. Is he not your lover, or did you go over there to find out nothing? I tell you, I came to save him, and to save him for you—no, not for you, you are not worth it, though he thinks you perfection! You are a wicked girl, and a fool! Come, come! why don't you speak? What has become of him? Is he over there now?"

Elsie was silent, but yielding. Fanny spoke again.

"Elsie—Elsie, speak—answer her! What happened over there, and where is the horse?"

Elsie turned to her, as though disdaining to answer Helen.

"Someone set his house on fire, I think; perhaps it was Jim, and Mr. Ticehurst has gone after him!"

"Ah!" said Helen, as if relieved, "if that is all! How did you know he is gone—did you see him, speak to him?"

"No," said Elsie; "I did not!"

"Then how do you know?" cried Fanny and Helen, together.

"There was a man there——"

Helen cried out as if she were struck, and Elsie paused.

"Go on!" the other cried—"go on!"

"And when I came up he was sitting by the house. I asked him if Mr. Ticehurst was there——"

"Oh, you fool!" groaned Helen, but only Fanny heard it.

"And he got up," continued Elsie, "and said there was no one there, but just as he was coming from his camp to see what the fire was, he heard a shot, and when he got to the house he saw somebody just disappear up the trail toward the cañon."

"Did you know him?" said Helen, as Elsie paused to take breath, for when she began to speak she spoke rapidly, and, conceal it as she would, it was evident she was in a fearful state of excitement.

"No," said Elsie; "but I think I have seen him before."

"Where is he, then?" cried Helen, holding her hand to her heart. "Is he there still?"

"No," cried Fanny, almost joyfully, "you gave him your horse to go and find Tom, and help him, didn't you, Elsie?"

And Helen screamed out in a terrible voice, "No, no! you did not, you did not—say you did not, girl!"

Elsie, who had turned whiter and whiter, turned to her suddenly.

"Yes, I did," she cried; "I did give him the horse."

Helen lifted her hands up over her head with an awful gesture of despair, and fell on her knees, catching hold of both the girls' dresses. But she held up and spoke.

"Oh, you wretched, unhappy girl!" she cried. "What have you done—what *have* you done? To whom did you give the horse? I know, I know! I saw him this very night—the man who swore to be revenged on him if it were after a century. The man who nearly killed him once, and who has escaped from prison. You have given him the means of killing your lover—you have given Tom Ticehurst up to Matthias, to a murderer—a murderer!"

And she fell back, and this time did not recover herself, but lay insensible, still holding the girls' dresses with as desperate a clutch as though she were keeping back from following me the man who was upon my track that terrible midnight. But Elsie stooped, freed her dress, and saying to Fanny, "See to her—see to her!" ran down to the stable again, just as her father rode through the higher gate.

And as that girl, who had known and ridden from her childhood, was saddling the first one she came to in the stable, I was riding hard and desperately in the dark not a quarter of a mile behind Siwash Jim.

The trail upon which we both were ran from my house, straight up into the mountains for nearly ten miles, and then followed the verge of the Black Cañon for more than a mile farther. When I came up to that place I stayed for one moment, and heard the dull and sullen roar of the broken waters three hundred feet beneath me, and then I rode on again as though I was as irresistibly impelled as they were, and was just as bound to cut my way through what Fate had placed before as they had been to carve that narrow and tremendous chasm in the living rock. And at last I came to a fork in the trail. If I had not been there before with Mr. Fleming, I should most likely have never seen Jim that night, perhaps never again. But we had stayed at that very spot. The left-hand fork was the main track, and led right over the mountains into the Nicola Valley; while the left and disused one, which was partially obliterated by thick-growing weeds, led back through the impassable scrub and rough rocks to the middle of the Black Cañon. I had passed that end of it without thinking, for indeed it was scarcely likely he would have turned off there. The chances seemed a thousand to one that Jim would take the left-hand path, but just because it did seem so certain, I alighted from my horse and struck a light. The latest horse track led to the right hand! He had relied on my taking the widest path, and continuing in it until it was too late to catch a man who had so skillfully doubled on me. I had no doubt that his curses at losing his revolver were changed into chuckles, as he thought of me riding headlong in the night, until my horse was exhausted, while he was returning the way I had come. I stopped to think, and then, getting on my horse, I rode back slowly to where the trails joined at the edge of the Cañon. I would wait for him there. And I waited more than half an hour.

It is strange how such little circumstances alter everything, for not only would Jim's following the Nicola trail have resulted in something very different, but, waiting half an hour, during which I cooled somewhat and lost the first blind rage of passion in which I had set out, set me reflecting as to what I should do. If I had come up with him at full gallop I should have shot him there and then. He would have expected it, and it would have been just vengeance; but now I was quietly waiting for him, and to shoot him when he appeared seemed to me hardly less cowardly conduct than his own. Then, if I gave him warning, he would probably escape me, and I was not so generous as to let him have the chance. Yet, in after years, seeing all that followed from what I did, I think I was more generous than just. I ought to have regarded myself as the avenging arm of the law, and have struck as coolly as an executioner. But I determined to give him a chance for his life, though giving him that was risking my own, which I held dear, if only for Elsie's sake; and so I backed my horse into the brush, where I commanded both trails, and, cocking both revolvers, I sat waiting. In half an hour I heard the tramp of a horse, though at first I could not tell from which way the sound came. But at last I saw that I had been right in my conjecture, and that my enemy was given into my hands. My heart beat fast, but my hands were steady, for I had full command over myself. I waited until he was nearly alongside of me, and then I spoke.

"Throw up your hands, Siwash Jim!" I said, in a voice that rang out over the roar of the waters below us, "or you are a dead man!"

And he threw them up, and as he sat there I could see his horse was wearied out. If it had not been, perhaps my voice would have startled it, and compelled me to fire.

"What are you going to do?" said he, sullenly peering in my direction, for he could barely see me against my background of trees and brush, whereas I had him against the sky.

"I will tell you, you miserable scoundrel!" I answered. "But first, get off your horse, and do it slowly, or I will put two bullets through you! Mind me!"

He dismounted slowly.

"Tie your horse to that sapling, if you will be kind enough," I said further;

"and don't be in a hurry about it, and don't attempt to get behind it, or you know what will happen."

When he had done as I ordered, I spoke again.

"Have you got any matches?"

"Yes," he replied.

"Of course you have, you villain! The same you set my house on fire with. Well, now rake up some brush, and make a little fire here."

"What for?" said he quickly, for I believe he thought for a moment I meant to roast him alive. I undeceived him if that was his idea.

"So that we can see each other," I replied, "for I'm going to give you a chance for your life, though you don't deserve it. Where's your six-shooter?"

"I dropped it," he grunted.

"And I picked it up," said I. "So make haste if you don't want to be killed with your own weapon!"

What his thoughts were I can't say, but without more words he set about making a fire, soon having a vigorous blaze, by which I saw plainly enough the looks of fear, distrust, and hatred he cast at me. But he piled on the branches, though I checked him once or twice when I thought he was going too far to gather them. When there was sufficient light to illuminate the whole space about us and the opposing bank of the cañon, I told him that was enough.

"That will do," I said; "go and stand at the edge of the cañon!"

He hesitated.

"You're not going to shoot me like a dog, and put me down there, are you?" said he, trembling.

"Like a dog?" said I passionately; "did you not try to smother me like a bear in his den, to burn me alive in my own house? Do as I tell you, or I'll shoot you now and roll your body in the river! Go!"

And he went as I asked him.

"Have you got any cartridges?" I demanded.

He pointed to his belt, and growled that he had plenty.

"Then stay there, and I will tell you what I will do with you. I am going to empty your revolver, and you can have it when it is empty. I will get off my horse and then you can load it again, and when I see you have filled it, you can do your best for yourself. Do you hear me?"

He nodded his head, and kept his eyes fixed on me anxiously, as though not daring to hope I was going to be so foolish as my word. But I was, even to the extent of firing his revolver into the air, though I had no suspicion of what I was really doing, nor what such an act would bring about.

I alighted from my horse, and let him go, for there was no danger of his running away. I even struck him lightly, and sent him up the trail out of the way of accident; and then, keeping my own revolver pointed at Jim, who stood like a statue, I raised his in my left hand. I fired, and the reports rang out over the hills. I threw Siwash Jim his weapon, saying:

"Load the chambers slowly, and count as you do so."

What a fool I was, to be sure, not to have shot him dead and let him lie! Though I should not have been free from the dangers that encompassed me, yet they would have been fewer, far fewer, and more easily contended with. But I acted as Fate would have, and even as I counted I heard Jim count too, in a strained, hoarse voice—one, two, three, four, five, six—and he was an armed man again, armed in the light, almost half-way between us, that glittered in his eyes and fell on my face. And it was his life or mine; his life that was worth nothing, and mine that was precious with the possibilities of love that I yet knew not, of love that was hurrying toward me even then, side by side with hate and death.

When Jim's weapon was loaded, he turned toward me with the barrel pointed to the ground. His eyes were fixed on mine, fixed with a look of fear and hatred, but hatred now predominated. I lowered my own revolver until we both stood on equal terms.

"Look," said I sternly; "you see that burning branch above the fire. It is already half burnt through; when it falls, look out for yourself."

And he stood still, perfectly still, while behind and under him the flood in the cañon fretted and roared menacingly, angrily, hungrily, and the sappy branch cracked and cracked again. It was bending, bending slowly, but not yet falling, when Jim threw his weapon up and fired, treacherous to the last. But his aim was not sure, no surer than mine when I returned his shot. As we both fired again, I felt a sting in my left shoulder, and the branch fell, slowly, slowly—ah! as slowly as Jim did, for he sank on his knees, rolled over sideways, and slipped backward on the verge of the cañon, its sloping, treacherous verge. And as he slipped, he caught a long root disclosed by the falling earth, and with the last strength of life hung on to it, a yard below me; as I ran to the edge, and stopped there, horror-struck. My desire for vengeance was satisfied, more than satisfied, for if I could have restored him to solid ground and life I would have done it, and bidden him go his way, so that I saw him no more. For his face was ghastly and horrible to see; his lips disclosed his teeth as he breathed through them convulsively, and his nostrils were widely distended. I knelt down and vainly reached out my hands. But he was a yard below me, and to go half that distance meant death for me as well. I knelt there and saw him fail gradually; his eyes closed and opened again and again; he caught his lower lip between his teeth and bit it through and through, and then his head fell back, his hands relaxed, and he was gone. And I heard the sullen plunge of his body as it fell three hundred feet into the waters below. I remained still and motionless for a moment. What a thing man was that he should do such deeds! I rose, and a feeling of sorrow and remorse for this terrible death of a fellow-creature made me stagger. I put my hand to my brow, and then peered over the edge of the cañon. What was I looking for? Was I looking into the river of Fate? I took my revolver and threw it into the cañon, that it should slay no other man. As it fell it struck a projecting rock, and, exploding, the echoes in the narrow space roared and thundered up the gorge toward the east, where, just beyond the mountains, the first faint signs of rosy dawn were written upon the heavens. Was that an omen of peace and love to me, of a fairer, brighter day? I lifted my heart above and prayed it might be so. But it was yet night, still dark, and the darkest hour is before the dawn, for as I turned my back to the cañon and stepped across to the fire which had lighted poor, foolish, ignorant Jim to his death, I looked up, and saw before me the thin face I feared more than all others, and the wicked eyes of my escaped enemy, Matthias of the *Vancouver*.

I have never believed myself a coward, for I have faced death too often, and but a few minutes ago I had risked my life in a manner which few men would have imitated; but I confess that in the horrible surprise of that moment, in the strange unexpectedness of this sudden and most unlooked-for appearance, I was stricken dumb and motionless, and stood glaring at him with opened eyes, while my heart's blood ran cold, For I was unarmed, by my own act of revulsion and remorse; and wounded too, for I could feel the blood trickle slowly from my shoulder that had been deeply scored by the second bullet from Jim's revolver. And I was in the same position that I had put him in, in a clear space with thick brush on both sides, through which there was no escape, and in which there was no shelter but a single tree to the left of the blazing fire, which was already gradually crawling in the dry brush. Surely I was delivered into my enemy's hands, for he was armed and carried a revolver, on whose bright barrel the fire glinted harshly. How long we stood facing each other I cannot say, but it seemed hours. If he had but fired then, he might have killed me at once, for I was unable to move; but he did not desire that, I could see he did not, as his hot eyes devoured me and gleamed with a light of savage joy and triumph. He spoke at last, and in a curiously quiet voice, that was checked every now and again with a sort of sob which made me shiver.

"Ah! Mr. Ticehurst," he said slowly, "you know me? You look as if you did. I am glad you feel like that. You are afraid!"

I looked at him and answered:

"It is a lie!"

And from that time forward it was a lie, for I feared no more.

"No," he said, "I think not; you are pale, and just now you shook. I don't shake, even after what I have been through. Look at me!"

He pointed his weapon at me, and his hand was as steady as a rock. He lowered it again and stroked the barrel softly with his lean left hand.

"You remember what I said to you," he went on, "don't you, Thomas Ticehurst? I do, and I have kept my word. Ah! I have thought of this many times, many times. They tortured me and treated me like a dog in the jail you sent me to; they beat me, and kicked me, and starved me, but I never complained, lest my time there should be longer. And when I lay down at night I thought of the time when I should kill you. I knew it would come, and it has. But just now, when I saw you by the side of your own grave, looking down, I didn't know whether it was you or the other man, and I thought perhaps he had killed you. If it had been he, I would have killed him."

He paused, and I still stood there with a flood of thoughts rushing through me. What should I do? If he had taken his eyes off mine for but one single moment I would have sprung on him; but he did not, and while he talked, I heard the horses champing their bits in the brush. And cruelest of all, my own horse moved, and put his head through the branches and looked at me. Oh, if I were only on his back! But I did not speak.

"How shall I kill you?" said Matthias at last; "I would like to cut you to pieces!"

He paused again, and then another horse that I had not yet seen moved on the other side of the trail where he had come up. It had heard the others, and I knew it must be the animal he had ridden. It came out of the brush into the light of the fire, and I knew it was Elsie's. My heart gave a tremendous leap, and then stood still. How had he become possessed of it? I spoke, and in a voice I could not recognize as my own, so hoarse and terrible it was.

"How did you get that white horse, you villain?" I asked.

He looked at me fiercely without at first seeing how he could hurt me, and then a look of beast-like, cruel cunning came into his eyes.

"Ah!" said he, "I knew her! It was your girl's horse! How did I get it? Perhaps you would like to know? You will never see her again—never! Where is she now—where?"

He knew as little as I did, but the way he spoke, and the horrible things he put into his voice, made me boil with fury.

"You are a lying dog!" I cried, though he had said nothing that I should be so wrathful. He grinned diabolically, seeing how he had hurt me, and then laughed loud in an insulting, triumphant manner. It was too much, and I made one tremendous bound across the fire, and landed within three feet of him. He fired at the same moment, and whether he had wounded me or not I did not know; but the revolver went spinning two yards off, and we grappled in a death-hug.

I have said that Siwash Jim was a hard man to beat, but whether it was that I was weak with my wound or not, I found Matthias, who was mad with hate and fury, the most terrible antagonist I had ever tackled. He was as slippery as an eel, as lithe as a snake, and withal his grip was like that of a steel trap. Yet if I could but prevent him drawing his knife, which was at his belt, I did not care. I was his match if not in agility, at least in strength, and I would never let him go. We were for one moment still, after we grappled, and I trust I shall never see anything that looks more like a devil than his eyes, in which the light of the fire shone, while he gnashed his teeth and ground them until the foam and saliva oozed out of his mouth like a mad dog's venom. His forehead was seamed and wrinkled, his cheeks were sucked in and then blown out convulsively, and his whole aspect was more hideous than that of a beast of prey. And then the struggle began.

At first it was a trial of strength, for although I was so much the bigger, he knew his own power and the force of his iron nerves, and he hoped to overcome me thus. We reeled to and fro, and twice went through the fire, where I once held him for an instant with a malicious joy that was short-lived, for the pain added to his strength, and he forced me backward, until I struck the trunk of the tree a heavy blow. Then we swayed hither and thither, for I had him by the right wrist and the left shoulder, not daring to alter my grip on his right hand, lest he should get his knife. He held me in the same way, and at last we came to the very verge of the cañon, and spurned the tracks that Jim had made in his agony. For a moment I thought he would throw us both in, but he had not lost hope. If he had, that moment would have been my last. In another second we had staggered to the fire, and he tried all his strength to free his right hand. At last, by a sudden wrench he did it, and dropped his fingers like lightning on his knife, just as I bent his left wrist over, and struck him in the face with his own clenched hand. We both went down; his knife ripped my shoulder by the very place that Jim's bullet had struck, and we rolled over and over madly and blindly, burning ourselves on the scattered embers, tearing ourselves on the jagged roots and small branches, which we smashed, as I strove to dash him on the ground, and he struggled to free his arm, which I had gripped above the elbow, to end the battle at one blow. But though he once drove the point more than an inch into the biceps, and three times cut me deeply, he did not injure any nerve so as to paralyse the limb. And yet I felt that I was becoming insensible, so tremendous was the strain and the excitement, and I felt that I must make a last effort, or die. Somehow we rose to our knees, still grappling, and if I looked a tithe as horrible as he did, covered with blood, saliva, and sweat, I must have been horrible to see. We glared in each other's eyes for one moment, and then, loosing my hold on his left arm, I caught his right wrist with both hands. With his freed hand he struck me with all his remaining strength full in the face while I twisted his right wrist with a force that should have broken it, but which only compelled him to relinquish the bloody piece of steel. And then we rolled over again, and lay locked in each other's arms. There was a moment's truce, for human nature could not stand the strain. But I think he believed I was beaten, and at his mercy, for he was on top of me, lying half across my breast, with his face not six inches from mine. He spoke in a horrible voice, that shook with hate and pain and triumph.

"I've got you now—and I'll kill you, as I did your brother!"

Great God! then it was he who had done it, after all. Better had it been for him to have held his peace, for that word roused me again as nothing else could have done, and I caught his throat with both hands, though he struck me viciously. I held him as he lay on top of me, and saw him die. Then I knew no more for a little while, and as I lay there insensible, I still bled.

What was it that called me to myself? Whether it was that my soul had gone out to meet someone, and returned in triumph, for I awoke with a momentary feeling of gladness; or whether it was an unconscious effort of the brain, in the presence of a new and terrible danger, I cannot say. All I know is that, when that spasm of joy passed, I felt weak and unable to move under the weight of Matthias, whose protruding eyes and tongue mocked at me hideously in death, as though his revenge was even now being accomplished; and I saw the fiery brush creeping across the space that lay between me and the fire Jim had kindled at my bidding. Was I to die by fire at the last, when that horrible night was passing and the dawn was already breaking on the eastern horizon? For I could not stir, my limbs were like lead, my heart beat feebly, and my feet were cold. I lay glaring at the fire, and, as I did so, I saw that the revolver I had struck out of Matthias's hand was lying as far from the fire as the fire was from me. How is it that there is such a clear intellect at times in the very presence of death? I saw then that the shots I had fired from that weapon had brought my enemy up just in time, for otherwise he might have been wearied out or lost; and now I thought if I could only get to it, to fire it, I might thus bring help: for what enemies had I left now save the crawling fire? I might even bring Elsie. But then, how did the dead villain who lay across me, choking me still, get her horse, and what had happened to her in his hands! I tried to scream, and I sighed as softly as the vague wind which was impelling the slow fires toward me. How near they came!—how near—and nearer yet, like serpents rearing their heads, spitting viciously as they came? And then I thought how slow they were; why did they not come and end it at once, and let me die? And I looked at the fires again. They were within two feet of me, I could feel the heat, and within eighteen inches of the revolver. I was glad, and watched it feverishly. But then the weapon's muzzle was pointed almost at me. Suppose it exploded, and shot me dead as it called for help! How strange it was! I put up my hands feebly and tried to move the dead body, so as to screen myself. I might as well have tried to uproot a tree, for I could barely move my hands. I looked at the fire again as it crawled on and on, now wavering, now staying one moment to lift up its thousand little crests and vicious eyes, and then stooping to lick up the grass and the dried brush on which I lay. But as I glared at it intently, at last it reached the weapon, and coiled round it triumphantly as though that had been its goal, licking it round and round. Would the flames heat the cartridges enough, and if they did, where would the bullets go? I asked that deliriously, for I was in a fever, and instead of being cold at heart, the blood ran through me like fire. I thought I began to feel the fire that was so close to me. I heard the explosion of the heated weapon. I was yet alive. "Come, Elsie! come, if you are not dead—come and save me—come!" I thought I cried out loudly, but not even her ear, that heard a sharper sound afar, could have caught that. Once more and once again the cartridges fired, and I heard a crash, saw a horse burst like a flame through the black brush, and there was a white thing before my eyes. I looked up and saw Elsie, my own true love after all, and then I fainted dead away, and did not recover until long, long after.

I ask myself sometimes even now, when those hours that were burnt into my soul return to my sight like an old brand coming out on the healed flesh when it is struck sudden and sharply, whether, after all, my enemy had been balked of his revenge. To die one death and go into oblivion is the lot of all who face the rising sun, and, after a while, veil their eyes when its last fires sink in the western sea. But I suffered ten thousand deaths by violence, by cruel ambush and torture, by crawling flames and flashing knives in the interval between my rescue and my recovery from the fever that my wounds and the horror of it all brought upon me. They told me—Elsie herself told me—that I lay raving only ten days; but it seemed incredible to me, as I shook my head in a vague disbelief that made them fear for my reason. If I had been in the care of strangers who were unfamiliar to me, I might have thought myself a worn-out relic of some dead and buried era, whose monuments had crumbled slowly to ashes in the very fires through which my soul had passed, shrieking for the forgetful dead I had loved. But though I saw her only vaguely like a spirit in clouds, or knew her, without sight as I lay half unconscious, as a beneficent presence only, I grew gradually to feel that Elsie, who still lived after the centuries of my delirium, loved me with the passion I had felt for her. I say *had* felt, for I was like a child, and my desire for her was scarcely more than a pathetic longing for tenderness of thought and touch, until the great strength which had been my pride returned in a flood and brought passion with it once more.

How strangely that came to pass which I had foretold in my last talk with Elsie! I had said, angrily—for I was angered—that she should one day speak to me, though she swore she would not, and that she should implore my pardon. And she did it, she who had been so strong and self-contained, in the meekest and dearest way the thoughts of a maiden could devise. And then she asked me if I would marry her? Would I marry her? I stared at her in astonishment, not at her asking, for it seemed the most natural thing in the world for her to do, but at the idiocy of the Question. "I do believe you love me, Elsie," I said at last, "for I have heard that love makes the most sensible people quite stupid. If you were in your right senses, dear, you would not have asked it——"

"I should think not, indeed!" she broke in. But she smiled tenderly.

"Because you know very well that I settled that long enough ago, on board the *Vancouver*," I said stoutly.

"Then I had no voice in it?" Elsie said.

"Not the least, I assure you! I made up my mind."

"And so did I," said Elsie, softly.

"What do you mean, dear?"

She leant her head against my shoulder, and against my big beard, and whispered:

"I made up my mind, dear Tom, that if you didn't love me, I would never love anyone else, but go and be a nun or a nurse all my life. And that's why

I was so hard, you know!"

Yes, I knew that well enough.

And where was Helen, meantime? I am drawing so near the end of my story that I must say what I have to in a few words. She had remained at the ranch until the doctor had declared I was going to recover (it was no fault of his that I did), and then she went away. What she told Elsie I have never known, nor shall I ever ask; but they parted good friends—yes, the best of friends—and she returned home to Melbourne. I never saw her again, at least not to my knowledge, although once, when Elsie and I were both in that city—for I returned to my profession—I thought, nay, for the moment I made sure, that she had come to know of our presence there. For Elsie had presents of fruit and flowers almost every day she was at Melbourne. I part with her now with a strange regret, and somehow I have never confessed to anyone that I was very vexed at her not waiting until I was well enough to recognize her before she went. For, you see, she loved me.

But—and this is the last—the time came when I was able to go out with Elsie and Fanny, and though we rode slowly, it did not need rapid motion to exhilarate me when she was by my side. As for Fanny, she used to lose us in the stupidest way, just as if she had not been brought up in the bush, and been able to follow a trail like a black fellow. But when Harmer came out on Sundays, it was we who lost them, for Fanny used to go off at full speed, while Jack, who never got used to a horse for many months, used to risk his neck to keep up with her. Then she used to annoy him at night by offering him the softest seat, which he stoutly refused, preferring to suffer untold tortures on a wooden stool, rather than confess. But I don't think they will ever imitate us, who got married at last in the autumn at Thomson Forks. I invited almost everyone I knew to the wedding, and I made Mac my chief man, much to Jack's disgust. I would even have invited Montana Bill, but he was lying in the hospital with a bullet in his shoulder; while Hank Patterson could not come on account of the police wanting him for putting it there. But half the population of the Forks had bad headaches next day; and if I didn't have to wear my right hand in a sling on account of the shaking it got, it was because I was as strong as ever. The only man who looked unhappy was Mr. Fleming, and he certainly had a right to be miserable, considering that I had robbed him of his housekeeper, leaving him to the tender mercies of flighty Fanny. And she was so vicious to poor Jack that he actually dared to say to me, "that if Elsie had the temper of her sister, he was sorry for me, and that it was a pity Siwash Jim and Mat had made a mess of it." When I rebuked him, he said merrily, "he guessed it was a free country, and not the poop of the *Vancouver*." So I let him alone, being quite convinced then, and I have never changed my opinion since, though we have been married almost five years, that Elsie Ticehurst is the best wife a man ever had, and worth fighting for, even against the world.

THE END

www.ingramcontent.com/pod-product-compliance
Ingram Content Group UK Ltd.
Pitfield, Milton Keynes, MK11 3LW, UK
UKHW020939280426
12138UKWH00036BA/475

9 781023 564243